CLAIM

Ruthless Billionaires

Aarti V Raman

ALSO BY AARTI V RAMAN

THE MILLIONAIRE FOE$

In Love With Her Millionaire Foe

In Debt To Her Millionaire Foe

Engaged To Her Millionaire Foe

In Bed With Her Millionaire Foe

Seducing Her Millionaire Foe

Deceived By Her Millionaire Foe

Betraying Her Millionaire Foe

Inherited By Her Millionaire Foe

A Millionaire Foes' Reunion

The Millionaire Foes Boxset (1-4)

The Millionaire Foes Boxset (5-8)

RUTHLE$$ BILLIONAIRE$

Claim

Keep

Burn

HER MERCENARY PROTECTOR

To Love Honor and Avenge

To Love Honor and Betray

FILTHY RICH GEEK$

Her Millionaire's Secret

Her Millionaire's Salvation

A Tale of Two Christmases

Her Millionaire's Secret

Her Millionaire's Redemption

A Filthy Rich Geek's Wedding

The Filthy Rich Geeks Boxset Collection

THOSE DANGEROUS ROYALS

Renegade

Chaos

A Night Out With Royals

STANDALONES

The Worst Daughter Ever

With You I Dance

Days Of Our Lives

Marrying Her Millionaire Foe

Something Old, Something New (Out of circulation)

DEDICATION

This book is dedicated to

Mom, my own True North.

Becca Syme who saved my career and my brain and my very life. You are a rockstar, Becca! THANK YOU.

The one and only, the inimitable Jackson Maine aka Bradley Charles Cooper. Drake has been you since I wrote one line about you in a book called Second Chance ten years ago.

A Devilish Lucifer for the crazy eyes.

Nashit and Beth, for being friends trusted and true.

My Kunju, my PM, Pudding's Amma who made the writing of this book possible on the fifth of June, 2021.

And the Big Guy in the Sky.

DRAKE & ANYA'S SOUNDTRACK

- o Every Breath You Take (feat. Tom Ellis & Debbie Gibson) By Lucifer cast, Tom Ellis, Debbie Gibson
- o Devil Devil By MILCK
- o In the Air Tonight By Jon Howard
- o Flood By Lhotse, Ellem
- o Shallow By Lady Gaga, Bradley Cooper
- o Can You Hear Me By UNSECRET, Young Summer
- o Creep (feat. Tom Ellis) By Lucifer Cast, Tom Ellis
- o Minefields By Faouzia, John Legend
- o Valkyrie By Battle Tapes
- o Kids By Robbie Williams, Kylie Minogue
- o Let's Go Out Tonight By The Blue Nile
- o My Love Will Never Die By AG, Claire Wyndham
- o Hallelujah By FVR DRMS
- o I Found By Amber Run
- o Not Your Hero By Becky Shaheen, Mally

*What could a man who has
everything possibly want? More.*

- Filthy Rich Vice Motto

Better to reign in hell,

Than serve in heaven

- Lucifer Morningstar,

John Milton's Paradise Lost.

PROLOGUE

Then

"You shouldn't have been born, boy."

The lash of the belt, the sharp sting of it, fell on a tender back. Not yet scarred by years of abuse and assault. The skin was still unmarred, not tough to stand the onslaught to come. Blood poured out, first in a trickle then in a steady stream, like a faucet leaking as the lashes rained down.

Like judgment.

Like death itself.

The monster who held the belt was tall. Taller than the tall mountain he climbed down every day in search of a job. But no one would hire a former tree logger who was a little too free with the booze bottle. And a little too careless with his two children.

He took his joblessness out on the two children under his care. When his booze ran out. When he went down the mountain. When he came back.

The lashes were ten, now.

Ten slick, sweaty, blood-soaked marks on a young boy's skin. The monster looked at the boy cowering at his feet, his hands curled protectively over his face, curved over himself, knees tucked into his chest so he presented the smallest possible target. The monster's dribble of spit fell on the boy's hair.

It smelled of hopelessness and despair. Of hate and weakness.

The spit, the shaming weight of it, more than the lashing, hardened the boy's heart. Cracked it into concrete poured onto a hard ground so nothing would ever grow.

"Say something, boy."

More spit, mixed with actual tears of rage plopped down the monster's chin. Landed on the boy's naked back. His shoulders. The salt of the tears burned his skin, scarring it. Unevenly. So that even years later, he'd not be able to look at his back without flinching.

"Say something."

The boy raised his eyes.

They burned.

Like hellfire and brimstone.

Like death itself, if death were an endless burning blue. Or the serene violence of a never-ending sky.

His eyes were a stunning electric blue scored against a raw, tanned face yet to settle into its bones.

They were a man's eyes.

And they refused to tear up. Even though the pain, the aching awful pain of the beating was beginning to make *itself known to him. In every rattling breath he took. In the seconds it took for him to raise his head.*

"What?" He croaked out. "Do you want me to say?"

The monster's belt hand trembled. "Say you're sorry. That you took her. That you're sorry you took her."

"I didn't," he shot back. "I didn't take her. You did."

"I wouldn't have taken her if…." The monster's massive chest heaved. As the sorrow and grief of losing the only person, the only creature he'd ever cared about, shot through him again. The pain weakening him again. Angering him again.

The boy's eyes burned and tears slid out. Salty and wasteful. He knew what was going to come. He braced a breath.

It didn't help.

The lash when it came stung twice as hard. Hurt four times as much.

It hurt every time for a long, long time.

But that night…when he looked into the monster's weak, pitiful face, he swore to himself he'd never rest, not for a minute till he built himself into the strongest monster alive. So that anyone who came for him, any creature big or small, would flee in his presence. Tremble from his wrath before it came.

He'd become the thing everyone feared.

Forever and always.

#####

Caleb Drake Fallahil sat up in a sweaty heave, as the tiny jitney boat rocked violently. The shadow of violence and sheer rage didn't entirely leave him as he switched on the tiny beside light he was allowed in his tiny room on the off-shore rig.

Once the room was lit, he turned to see outside the porthole and saw nothing but inky black sky. Then he squinted. He could make out the jagged peaks of lightning. The thunder and rain lashing the boat trickled down into his consciousness.

The door to his cabin blasted open.

"How bad is it?" Drake asked the first mate. "Why didn't you wake me?"

"We tried to wake you. You punched Riggs in the mouth, two hours ago. We figured we'd let you sleep it off."

The first mate was named Klien, a short Nordic man who spoke with a flat accent and was a genius with cards. He'd taught Drake everything he knew about counting cards after he regularly cleaned him out at Friday night Texas Hold 'Em. Now, Klien handed Drake an orange inflatable jacket and watched as he strapped it on.

Drake was a young god in the making. Tall and golden and beautifully made, with the curling hair to match. Although it was dyed an ashy black right now.

He had raw boned strength, a plus on any off-shore rigging operation. He could keel the lines while maintaining the cylinders for two days straight without missing a single inspection or check.

And he could single-handedly haul the drums of crude deposit in his two arms when they were short-handed on the cranes. But that was more because he was a stubborn bastard who wouldn't allow anyone to outdo him in contests of strength.

"I'll apologize to Riggs later. How bad is it?"

~~~~~

Klien ran out of Drake's small cabin. It was distressingly bare of any personal effects. But that was to be expected. The boy was only eighteen. He'd probably come from a bad family situation and needed no reminders of the life he'd left behind.

"It's a Type 2. They're calling it a cyclonic storm, extended. We're required to batten down the hatches."

"Where's everyone?"

"The captain's trying to disperse everyone to the safest areas. It's not a big operation but we need the rig secured…" Klien trailed off, apologetically, looking up at the younger man.

He was quiet, meditative.

"It wasn't this bad two hours ago," Klien continued. "When Riggs came to wake you up."
~~~~~

"When I punched him." Drake twisted his knuckles as if to check for damage. He couldn't find any.

"Yes. We let you sleep in till we couldn't. What were you dream…it sounded bad in there, Drake," Klien sounded softly.

"It was hell," Drake said flatly. "But I woke up. And I'm here."

Klien gave him yet another apologetic look as they rounded the wet galley kitchen and came above decks. Huge searchlights placed men scurrying about in little orange vests. Away from the center of the noise and commotion of the enormous drilling rig making the company they worked for supremely, incredibly wealthy.

"Could you…?"

"I'll take the drums and cylinders. Shut off the valve," Drake decided. "You guys hold the rest."

Drake took off in the direction of where the combustible materials of the engine and the drilling equipment were kept. Walking right into the heart of the storm. Into the heart of the very beast that might blow him up to kingdom come. His orange vest a small fading beacon in the lashing rain and thunder.

He was a man among men, Klien thought to himself.

Or a monster.

ONE

❖

Now

FILTHY RICH VICE

Hello Sneak Peakers,

Have you missed me? Because I've missed you.

The first order of business would be to inform…no… **proclaim** *that the imposter who snatched Toast of The Town! and held it to ransom has been apprehended and is now languishing in a prison far, far away from our fair shores. But, this does mean that the golden name of ToTn! and reputation of this good scribe has been called into question.*

While I can do little but allow for time to heal all wounds reputation-wise, I can do something about the name.

What's in a name you ask? Everything, darlings.

After careful consideration and much deliberation, I've decided to retire the ToTn! moniker digitally, socially, online and offline. It's time for a rebrand.

Hell, it's time for a game-changing pivot. We are going global, people.

And I'm going to be everywhere you aren't, Peakers. Everywhere you want to be. Giving you sneak peeks of how the rich, the ruthless, the powerful live their lives. How they make their sordid deals and lie on their gilt-soft beds while we slave to swell their billionaire bottom-lines.

I'm going to expose their depraved hearts, Peakers. The demons they've worked the hardest to hide.

And they're going to be helpless when I do so.

And you? You're going to love me for it.

Welcome to Filthy Rich Vice. The price of entry is a decadent secret you won't tell the world.

This is the last post on this website. I'll be back with a spanking-new online real estate sooner than you can say lobster-fed Kobe beef served on five hundred dollar duck pate reared in Her Majesty's Gardens herself.

Xx

Me

PS: Click on this link to see exclusive pictures of this billionaire VC in hiding, sunning with the next Leonine Princess herself atop the Marina Bay Sands Infinity Pool. Yes, this blogger has confirmed those are *her real assets his ham-size hand is covering. Drake Fallahil, you didn't think you could live in obscurity forever, did you?*

THIS SITE IS UNDER CONSTRUCTION. SIGN UP HERE TO BE NOTIFIED WHEN IT GOES LIVE.

~ ~ ~ ~ ~ ~ ~

She was going to break Drake Fallahil.

Or she was going to break up with him.

Aster Chan was a flower of the finest quality, she was Singaporean royalty, without being actually related to the Royal Family. She was beautiful with ash-grey eyes arched under lush brows, perfect cheekbones and an impressive figure maintained through diet and exercise and the occasional cosmetic help. She was also fucking *smart.*

Don't ask her. Ask the Dean of Harvard University who'd offered her a chair, a *permanent* chair in the economics department of the most prestigious business school in the whole fucking world.

Or the Chairman of an unnamed Forbes 500 company who'd wanted her to take over as Chief Financial Officer so their profits could grow hundred times like she'd shown him they could over a damn cocktail napkin last weekend when he'd come over for dinner at her Ah-ma, her grandmama's, place on Turong Road.

She had wealth, breeding, and opportunities galore. She'd tragically wasted it all on the one man who'd refused to break for her.

Aster brooded as the water lapped gently over her perfect size thirty-six D breasts. The tips a sweet blushing pink, barely visible over the sudsy water.

Tonight they were going to have the mother of all showdowns.

And tonight, for once, the famed investor who never placed a losing bet – on the stock market, at the startup table or on a game of chance - was going to lose.

Aster smiled, a brittle smile. Her sloe-shaped eyes hard and calculative that absolutely belied her softness and charm. It perfectly suited the moniker of Leonine Princess that wretched blogger had slapped on her.

The double doors to the bath suite – for it was a suite – shushed open. For, room was too small a word for the space that held the cream-colored bathroom and toilet furnishings and fittings. The waterfall shower, the heart-shaped recessed Jacuzzi which was just the right side of tacky, and the actual rainforest supertrees of the Gardens by The Bay providing one solid wall of the highest apartment in the tallest tower in all of Singapore.

Then there was the piece de resistance, the free standing bathtub, hauled from the palaces of a defunct Bedouin sheik, with real gold inlaid stubby legs. The tub reigned on a dais of its own as if it was king of all it surveyed, with a skylight above showcasing more of the stunning Gardens skyline.

It was a lush, verdant, forest-like atmosphere more in keeping with a resort in the Saharan wilderness than in the penthouse apartment of the most elite addresses in one of the most sought-after countries in the world.

Aster lounged against the lip of the tub, artfully positioned against the clever (not smart, clever) lighting in the bathroom that was always set to, *haha,* Jungle. Soft, intimate, slightly predatory.

She knew the slender line of her perfectly proportioned body was displayed to the best advantage. The lavender suds of the bath bomb were just beginning to dissipate leaving a slightly steamy mist around her face, softening her curls and scenting her body. Preparing her for her lover.

Her lover…who regarded her with watchful eyes.

He didn't step inside.

~ ~ ~ ~

"You know what pisses me off?" Aster asked conversationally, trailing water over scented, painted fingers.

"What?" Drake asked back, equally casually.

Aster felt her whole body tighten at his casual dismissal. At the bored tone and the easy, relaxed stance of this man who was built like a fucking lumberjack. Or an offshore rig worker.

Drake didn't have a deep voice. It wasn't a baritone, like her dear Papa, or her brother Jacob. Deep and commanding.

But Drake's voice was hypnotic. It begged you to follow him to whatever unplumbed depths of excess he wanted you to join him in. Drake's voice was *lethal.*

"That that wretched blogger wouldn't have gotten off a shot of me, topless, if you'd had a PR team managing your life."

"I don't like my life being managed, Aster," he said, quietly.

"Then, at the very least, we should have been sunning here. In this gorgeous bathtub. Instead of slumming it at the Marina Sands."

Drake cocked his head. He still wore his work clothes, a full three-piece suit in corded steel with just the midnight blue tie crooked. The only sign of dishabille he permitted himself. Even every inch of his wavy, curling hair was in place as it had been when he'd brushed it in the morning.

She knew, because he'd done so at her apartment at Jurong Park.

"Your point being, Aster?"

Aster took a deep breath. It did interesting things to her breasts. She hoped his electrifying eyes were trained on them. She liked to think of his eyes on her breasts. "The point being, I'm a Chan, Fallahil. Of The Singapore Chans. Family names mean something here. We can't be…sullied in public on a gossip website."

"I'm sorry, my dear." Drake inclined his golden head, except his hair wasn't really golden. Even though magazine articles had described him as The Golden God Midas from top to toe, his hair was more a burnished gold, like crests of brown shot through with gilt edges. "I have done everything short of calling a bounty on the head of this Filthy Rich Vice blogger person. I don't know what else you want me to do to mitigate this inconvenience."

"*Inconvenience?*"

Aster rose up, Minerva rising up from the foaming waters of Jupiter's head. The single lotus flower she'd strategically placed near her navel slid down her belly and down her thighs.

To her raging disappointment, Drake's eyes stayed level on her stunning, enraged face.

"My family and I have been humiliated by my association with you, Drake," she hissed out. A tendril of her perfect black hair slid down her cheek and she blew it away angrily.

Drake's eminently kissable lips twitched at the action.

"My Ah-ma is heartbroken. My dad nearly had an apoplexy when he saw his business partner chuckling at my...my *breasts*...on display on that vulgar site. Not to mention, whatever business prospects I might have had took a severe hit with what that wretched blogger wrote about me."

"She didn't lie, you know." Drake unbuttoned his jacket, the movement brisk and competent. "I'd take it as compliment if I were you. She called these ham-sized." He held up his palms. And they were perfectly square, large, in proportion with his six-three height.

His hands were rough and callused with ridges under the bases of the fingers, from whatever he'd done in his early years. And they knew how to bring her to screaming, quivering orgasm.

"Don't prevaricate," Aster snapped.

Drake held his palms up. "I wouldn't dream of it, Aster. How can I make it up to you?"

Aster smiled. A cobra hooking its next victim. "Would you, really? Would you, if it were in your power to make it up to me?"

Drake nodded, slowly. Unblinking. He too knew what it was to look a dangerous predator in the eye. He was the most dangerous of them all. "If it was within my power then I'd love to. I'm a generous man, sweetheart."

Drake grinned. A flash of teeth against golden skin, with lines fanning from the corners of his eyes to the edge of his temples. A man who smiled a lot, was quite comfortable with it. Reveled in it.

But then, he'd taken over companies and made ungodly sums of money betting on the most ridiculous advancements in tech and innovation, all while smiling like he loved nothing but a good time. A beach bum who'd just lucked into the good life.

Then you saw his eyes. And they were...blank.

Utterly smoothly blank.

As if the man didn't know how to laugh.

Aster stepped out of the tub.

And Drake was right there, next to her. In a sudden, slick movement that was soundless and a little scary if she was being honest about it. But she attributed her jacked up heart rate to the rush of adrenalin. Of making this invincible man break at her feet.

He handed her down the four steps of the marble dais and wrapped her in a lush organic cotton robe that clung wetly, seductively to every single inch of her sculpted body.

His expression was meditative.

Aster stepped forward, touched Drake's chest. It was hot. Furnace-hot. As if his heart was trying to beat its way out of his impressive chest.

"Marry me." She spoke throatily.

Her eyes were earnest and wide, her lips were lush and full and unpainted. She was at her sexy, devastating best. Nude. Perfect. Wrapped in a robe that hid nothing. That showed him what belonged to him, what had since he'd landed up in the land of the Sea Lion a year ago with nothing but two suitcases full of work dockets.

The suitcases had swelled to six now but she'd never doubted they belonged together.

"Marry me, Drake. Make an honest woman out of me. And let's give this thing between us a real shot. You know I'm perfect for you."

She gripped his jacket with each word she spoke, punctuated each word with a soft kiss on his jaw. His beard tickled her nose but she kept her sneeze in. This was a moment of power. Of romance.

"Aster…"

"Marry me, Drake. No one knows you like me. Definitely not in this city, if not in the world."

Drake blinked, once. A rapid movement of his eyes. That was a landed shot.

Aster pressed her body closer, offering herself to him. Drenching him with her heat, the wetness of her bath, the lavender scent of the bath bomb. "With my family's connections and your considerable wealth, we can rule over Singapore for the next fifty years."

Drake unwrapped her fingers from his jacket, peeling them off one by one. "That's what it is, isn't it?" He still spoke casually.

As if they were discussing dinner preferences or the weather. Or the NASDAQ500.

"You want to cement your place in the echelons of this city. And the world, I presume."

"What's wrong with wanting greatness? Don't you chase it yourself, Drake?"

"I do," he agreed without a qualm. "I don't fuck my way into it, though."

Aster slapped him.

The sound echoed in the gentle streams of music echoing in the room.

~ ~ ~ ~ ~

Drake's cheek burned from the force of Aster's slap. His head tipped back from the reverb of the movement. And for a single, blinding second, he was a seven-year-old scrawny kid in St. Cloud, Minnesota, being backhanded by Caleb Timothy Fallahil before the belt came out.

For a single, blinding second he considered slapping her back. Marring all that perfect, unblemished, expensively-maintained skin with the strength of his fury.

Her eyes widened, something akin to fear making them skitter over his face and eyes.

His mask came back. Slid into place. He smiled once more, feeling the lines stretch and slide all over his face. Pull into his skull. "I'm sorry. That was badly done of me. I'm sorry, Aster."

"Don't apologize if you don't mean it, Fallahil," she snapped. Some of her original fire coming back to heat her up. "And you never mean it."

"I did mean it this time." He gripped her elbow. The wet cloth rapidly heated under his touch. "I'm sorry. I have been screwing this up for some time, haven't I?"

Aster huffed out a breath that made it very hard for him to keep his eyes pointed north. Then she visibly softened and leaned into him. And he was wary. Aster was soft only when on the hunt, either in the boardroom or elsewhere.

It was what had attracted her to him. They were the same. Predators.

"No. Not entirely. I just…Oh, Drake." She was distressed. "My family is threatening to disown me if we don't fix this blogger problem. You know how my grandmamma is."

Oh, he well knew how clannish and traditional the Chinese-Singaporeans were. How they had liberal, Western business values which underscored their very traditional, extremely familial values. He respected their culture, as much as he could a culture he'd more or less intended to buy his way into, but the Chans were old-school in a lot of ways.

In business. And family.

Aster was their golden child. The girl who'd excelled at everything she put her mind to, whose final accomplishment would be mating with a man of suitable bearing, status, and net worth.

He wondered with a bite of real humor if she knew he'd literally been born aboard a Zamboni on the highway between Minnesota and Nebraska.

"I do." He smiled, placating her. "And I'll come and explain the whole situation to her. I'll buy out her favorite florist and that dumpling place she enjoys so much – Sue Kang's. I'll help make it right for you, Aster." It was the least he could do, after that ridiculous blogger had come after Aster to get to him.

Her lips quivered and Drake's blood stirred. Despite himself. Despite what he'd told himself he'd do when he saw her next.

Break it off.

They had run their course, now it was time to put things back on an even keel. Even without the salacious gossip item, he'd known she was going to make some kind of demand from him.

And he was going to have to let her down easy.

"Aster…"

"Why won't you just agree to marry me? It's not like you have anyone else lined up for you. Not like anyone will tolerate your…your…insomnia and bouts of darkness as I do."

"Didn't know it was such a hardship to keep me occupied in the night, sweetheart," he drawled.

"It's not like anyone else will *have* you, Drake," she continued, taunting him. With her face, her voice, her nails raking a path down his skin. Over it. Enflaming him. In more ways than one.

"How do you know that?" he deadpanned. "All the media publications agree I'm a catch. I'm the uncatchable catch."

Her eyes flipped to his. Cobra-sharp and just as deadly. All the playfulness left her body. Her face. "Well, I caught you. In public. On the internet, no less."

"Gossip sites are not worth the effort anymore, sweetheart. You're going to have to do better than that to catch me."

"I don't want to catch you," she spat out. "I wanted to offer you me."

"And I respectfully declined."

"You don't get to do that." She poked one taloned nail at his tie. Almost breaking the suit open in her fury. "To me."

Suddenly, he was tired. Exhausted, actually. It had been a long day, finalizing the premises of his company's new headquarters in the most coveted address in the city – Aura Smart City's Oceania Park. It was a temporary co-working space he'd leased in entirety till they figured out how to build the campus he wanted built here – one that was smart, sustainable, and his favorite able – profitable.

He wanted whatever drama this was, over and done with.

Then he wanted to sleep, for a change.

"Fine. I don't," he agreed amiably. "You can play it however you want to your friends and family, Aster. Tell them I begged you on bended knees to marry me and you refused me because I was too plebian for your standards. Tell them I can't get it up. I don't care anymore."

Silence greeted his final words.

For a second, he thought she'd hit him again. And he wasn't sure he had control left enough to not hurt her back.

Then her face crumpled. "You really don't care, do you?"

He ran a hand down his aching face. Fuck, he needed a drink. "I'm sorry, Aster."

He didn't want to hurt her. But... "We made no promises to each other, save exclusivity. And I've been faithful to you for as long as we've been together. That is all I can give you."

"That is all?" she repeated. "After all the time and energy I invested in you…in us. That is *all?* No, Drake Fallahil. That is not all. That is most certainly not all."

"Fine. What do you want?" Drake snapped out. His voice cold and foreboding. "What the fuck do you want, Aster? A board position in my company or an introduction to my pals at the yachting club? Maybe someone else will…"

He caught her hand before it flashed up and struck him a second time. His hold was light, impersonal. Implacable. "Don't. Not again." He spoke softly but the intent was clear in his eyes.

"I want to bet you ten million dollars," Aster said softly. "That in three weeks' time, you'll beg me to marry you. Because no one else will have you anywhere in this country. And if I win…you'll marry me and we'll move away for good from Singapore."

His head snapped back. "You don't mean that."

He was cool, purposeful. Business-like. But the blood hummed beneath his Brioni jacket and suit. It flickered into flames like it always did when money, when luck, chance, and fortune opened their maws wide and invited him to walk into them and walk back out alive.

"You *don't* mean that, Aster. Be reasonable."

"Are you afraid of losing, Fallahil?"

She'd asked the most damaging question of them all. "Aster, don't be ridiculous."

"I'm deadly serious. We'll even have our attorneys draw up an agreement." She smiled, exposing neat white teeth. Poised to strike like a tiny shark. "We can call it my bride price. We're old-fashioned that way."

"I'm not marrying you in three weeks, woman."

"Then prepare to move. Tonight. In a city as small as mine, all it needs is one well-placed rumor for all the doors to shut in your face, Drake. Personal…and business." She ran a nail down his sleeve. "My name carries a lot more weight than some random blogger's yet."

"Why do you want to punish me for the gossip piece in some two-bit website no one's ever heard of, Aster?"

Aster shrugged. A delicate, female movement. "Because you're handy. Because you are the great and mighty Drake Fallahil, who's moved across two continents in the hopes of conquering it. Take your pick."

"That's not…I don't want to conquer anything, Aster." He tried to voice the protest but it didn't entirely hold true.

Yes, he'd stepped down from actively managing his vast company, only narrowing his focus down to the VC hedge fund, his very first business venture.

And yes, relocating to Singapore was a purely fiscal decision. It was the city of the future. The only city worth the astronomical prices he'd paid for the whole move – buying property, establishing a base, hiring a plethora of locals across Asia, Southeast and Far East, legitimizing the Fallahil name as covertly as he could.

"You don't?" She was faintly scornful.

"I could move tomorrow. I am not particularly attached to this place yet." He looked calculatedly around the bathroom that was, end-to-end, larger than the off shore rig he'd spent his late teens and early twenties in. It flickered nothing in him. Not pride. Not satisfaction.

Yes, he wasn't attached at all.

"Then do it."

And there she had him. Because it was the principle of the thing. He'd given his word about the move, to his people, to the people who wanted to work with him… and he didn't renege on his word.

Drake thought rapidly, weighed the odds. Figured he could literally import a bride…

"You can't mail-order one from the States or anywhere else. She has to be from here." Aster nixed his bright idea in the bud.

"You're not going to let this go? You want to drag this out for another three weeks?"

"I want to make you understand what you should have already." She kissed his cheek. "I'm yours," she said softly. "You're mine."

"I belong to no one, Aster." He moved away from her gently, as if she was a ticking time bomb. "I never will."

"Then you should have no problem placing this bet."

She'd called him out one too many times and dammit, the hassle of actually moving HQ again after shifting everything piece by piece over the last one year was unthinkable. Not to mention, aggravating.

She couldn't win. Not Aster Chan.

"Fine." He held out his hand. "I agree to the terms of your stupid bet. If I win, you hand over ten million dollars *and* I stay here. If you win, I'll marry you and stay here. If I can't find anyone else, I'll move away from Singapore. Does that satisfy you?"

She cupped his erection, poking shamelessly through the cut of his flat-front pants. "Not even close. But I will be. In three weeks. Lover."

Then Aster Chan dropped the robe she'd worn to the most-important negotiation of her life and exited the bath suite as magnificently naked as the day she'd been born.

Leaving Drake drooling after her.

As her intention was, he mused tiredly. And the thing was, he couldn't even blame her for it. This was the most interesting bet he'd made in his life.

One he had no intention of losing. Not to a monster like her.

TWO

Sixteen days later…

"I used to hear this happened in Harvard," one of the girls, Nonita, giggled as she refreshed her wine-red, blowjob-ready lipstick. "They would bus in these girls from the nearby colleges – BU and the like – all for the privilege of sleeping with the next powerful man in business from the Final Clubs. They'd call it the Fuck Bus."

Anya Mallya-Bhatt flinched as she heard the crude term.

The girls around her burst out laughing. They didn't feel offended at the term or the fact that they were traveling in a similar vehicle, a small tastefully decorated bus, which held about forty beautifully attired girls — ranging from blond, brunette to true redheads and all the shades under the sun. They were all of legal age, of course, but they looked no older than nineteen.

"I like it," one of the other girls declared. She did a quick shimmy on the nearest pole. The slit in her cheongsam riding high, revealing a gleaming white garter encasing her thigh. "We ride the Fuck Bus."

Anya pressed herself straight against the last seat. Wishing she could be anywhere but here. Enduring this depraved and humiliating experience, for the sake of a promise she shouldn't have had to make in the first place.

She had exams coming up next week. An important paper on the Ethics of International Finance that she had to research for. She didn't actually have *time* to be on the goddamn fuck bus.

But here she was.

Anya watched as the bus took a turn of Tanjong Pagar and entered the elite part of the fair country she called home. Tanjong Pagar was an upscale neighborhood, gentrified by startup billionaires who showed up here in the last twenty years, right when Singapore welcome tech and innovation with both arms and legs.

The difference in the neighborhood became noticeable, even though it was after eleven pm and most of the restaurants and cafes were shutting down. Leaving just the late-night ones open.

On one side were the cute and kitschy shops, maintained by a beautiful sidewalk, where ordinary folk ordered their turmeric chai lattes and tomato and egg ramen noodles, unwinding after a long week at work.

And, then, on this side, the side of the bus were the tall skyscrapers – chrome and steel monstrosities covered by vertical gardens to maintain the Smart Green City tag. These office spaces and residences had sprung up around the time the new billionaires showed up, adapting to the chic and quaint pace of Singapore faster than anyone ever gave them credit for.

Like monolithic gods towering to the sky, as if they belonged there more than the ordinary folks ever could.

On this side of the road Lexuses and Jags dotted the road, zooming at ungodly speeds toward the ritzier Friday night spots.

On this side of the road, wealth and class mingled quietly with each other to create untold wealth and dynasties that were just beginning to emerge.

It was as if an invisible line divided the six-lane freeway. And she supposed it was foolish to resent people to spend the money they had earned however they wished.

Even on a fuck bus, Anya took a quick look around the scented and glammed up dolls she spared bus space with. Each of them were total stunners in their own way. Some were runway model tall, others were busty and curvy in all the right places and all of them were eager for a good time.

After all, the casting agency they'd all been sent by had promised hefty bonuses on top of the per diem if the hosts were happy.

This was apparently a very special party. A once-in-a-blue-moon kind of event. Hosted by the Runwal Brothers, big-shot property developers whose family had made a killing gentrifying the neighborhood the bus was racing along.

The Runwal Brothers were the only reason Anya was on this goddamn bus.

~ ~ ~ ~ ~ ~

"What's your name, honey?"

"An..Anika," Anya husked out an answer to the kindly, sweating blond who'd swung into the empty seat next to her. She held her hand out and the blond shook it delicately.

"Hey, Anika. I'm Tonya." She gave a big smile to go with the introduction and nodded at the girls congregated at the front of the bus. Music pumped out of someone's sound bar and they were all bumping and grinding over it. "Silly, aren't they?"

Anya gave her a tight smile but said nothing.

"This is your first time," Tonya said accurately taking a puff of her vape pen. "I can see it. The tight eyes. The stiff posture." She patted Anya's stocking-clad knee.

Who the fuck wore sheer black stockings in high eighties humidity? Women who were intent on seducing fat, slobbering drunks who had more money than sense, that's who.

"It's so obvious."

Anya's smile stretched wider, became paper thin at the edges. "We all have to start somewhere, don't we?"

"We do." The blond gave a considering puff. "You don't get your cut if you don't come inside. Estella Martin, our coordinator needs to see the stamp on our wrist before the money gets deposited in our account."

"I wasn't thinking of running for it," Anya protested.

Liar, her ego mocked her. *You were plotting your escape from the fuck bus. You hold these women in contempt. And want to protect them at the same time.*

"I won't blame you if you do. Some of these events…" Tonya gave a delicate shudder and leaned in close as if to impart a state secret. "I've seen fight clubs enacted in the basements of one of the Good Class Bungalows on Great Albert."

She named *the* most exclusive address in the whole world, and definitely in Singapore. Where property wasn't just owned, it was handed down from generation to generation. Usually to sons with Roman numerals after their names.

"These people are sick. In the fucking head," Tonya said bluntly. "But they pay well. So we do what we do."

Anya swallowed a hot spurt of fear and anger at the idea of an underground fight club existing anywhere in the world at all. A place where men pummeled each other without rules or decency for the enjoyment of rich fucks who had nothing better to do than bet on their outcomes.

It was heinous.

"We do what we do," she echoed quietly.

She was no better than any of these women, not really. They had their own reasons to be here on this bus. Maybe it was money, maybe it was the idea of clinging to transferred power, fucking it, really. Maybe they were desperate and couldn't get another job anywhere.

Who was she to judge them?

"That's better." Tonya patted Anya's cheek.

It was hot to the touch. Possibly from the stupid stockings she had been forced to wear. Mostly from all the red-hot anger of enduring the indignities of the night.

"Get pissed off. Use them. Like they're using us," she advised Anya.

Then she swung away to join the crowd of partying girls in the front with a wink and a smile to Anya.

The bus swung into the basement parking structure of a behemoth skyscraper called Luxor Apartments.

The Runwals owned the top ten floors of the structure, where they lived and worked. Mostly.

This was the intel she'd been provided. And her source was not wrong about these kinds of details.

The girls exited one by one, straightening their clothes and checking their reflections one last time on the camera apps of their phones. The air was palpable with excitement and danger and healthy lust.

Tonya, you have no idea, Anya thought grimly as she squeezed into the middle of the last batch. Determined to make herself as nondescript as it was possible to be. And since she wasn't built like a goddamn gazelle, it was very possible.

~ ~ ~ ~ ~

"Name?" The burly security expert, dressed in trademark black with a cream earpiece, checked an enormous clipboard as he looked dispassionately at her. He only saw what she wanted him to see.

A dark-haired, petite woman with three buttons undone on her bowrrwed waitress's uniform. And the damned stockings, of course.

"Anika Jalan," Anya said smokily. She presented the ID she'd been given just for tonight, procured from a seedy photographer's studio in Mohammad Market. The fake ID was her idea but the name was a dirty joke played on her.

The man scanned her ID on the tablet screen. It blinked green in a flash.

"Right hand, please."

Anya held her hand out. Another guard, this one dressed more like a door guard, in epaulets and livery smiled widely, toothily as he took a needle-like thing and pressed the plunger against the lip of an ink bottle.

Anya blinked. What the fuck? No one had said anything about a tattoo.

"It's a temporary tattoo," he explained in accented English. Still giving her that same toothy smile. "It should wash away in two days."

Anya saw that his pupils were blown. This man was high, on ketamine, from the looks of it, since he was functional.

Her insides writhed at what she had been reduced to. But she nodded and gave him an unconcerned smile. "I'm scared of needles." It was a half-truth.

The boy, for he really couldn't be older than twenty-three, produced a blue pill. "Take this. You won't feel a thing," he promised her.

Anya's heart stopped. But the hand she held out to take the pill was rock-steady. She placed it against the tip of her tongue and folded it underneath, determined not to breathe the foul thing in.

This night had turned into a living nightmare, and it had not even begun.

The boy gently pressed the plunger against the inside of her wrist, right where green veins snaked up to her palm. He traced the design of a closed lotus flower sitting on its own pad, perfectly and flawlessly over her hand.

She felt each press of the needle against her skin but remained unmoved, casually relaxed.

When he was done he gently pressed a kiss against the dark, almost bluish ink and winked up at her. "There. All done."

"Thank you, sweetie."

Anya slipped out of the booth near the elevator. Her hand throbbing faintly from the gentle pressure of the needle. Heart pounding, determination and anger flicking at her veins.

She was the last one to board the elevator. Then it closed on her, and she was enclosed in a space with ten other women – perfumed and dressed to within an inch of their lives.

The elevator began its slow descent up.

Anya clenched her freshly tattooed hand. It hurt. But that was good. Her eyes burned with unshed tears, she forced back with each swallow of breath. She needed the pain to remind her of her mission tonight. Or she'd just whip out her phone and record the hedonism on display tonight and post it on social media, let the filth fall where it may.

Then she'd see how the NASDAQ 500 survived.

The elevator doors opened. A pleasant-faced matron in a tasteful cheongsam held a velvet tray. "No cell phones beyond this point, ladies."

The women placed their phones on the tray. Anya included.

Once they'd all been divested of their phones and scanned for weapons of any kind by a special scanner, the lady smiled benignly at them. As if she was doing them a favor.

"Welcome to Bacchanalia." She pressed a button on the wooden wall behind her. Like magic, Alladin's freaking cave, it split open to reveal a glass wall.

In fact, Anya could see that the whole penthouse was surrounded by a thirty-foot glass wall. As if there existed no barrier between sea and sky and this little place hung in space by human will alone. Under other circumstances she'd have been excited, thrilled to tears to visit this beautiful piece of architectural design.

The thumping bass should have shattered the wall but it held. People milled about, dressed in their designer finest, holding glasses of champagne. As if this was nothing more than a weekend high society event.

But it wasn't.

It was Bacchanalia. Where anything and everything went. Where these people worshipped their basest desires and fed on it through money and power and the influence holding this city together.

As it was, her gaze sharpened, hardened. She caught side of the man she'd come to see tonight.

Ajay Runwal.

Anya was expelled out of the elevator. She stepped through the magic glass wall and into the home of the man she hated the most in the world.

THREE

Drake was bored.

He swirled the olive in his dirty martini, the vermouth sliding down cold and easy, he contemplated the exact nature of his boredom.

Was it the company tonight? This hedonistic lot with their designer gowns and twenty-thousand dollar suits and Beluga caviar served on duck's eggs, barely able to fill his appetite, now that he remembered to eat at least two whole meals a day.

He wanted to be at home with these people – the Who's Who of the social set in the city he wanted to *own*.

He wore the clothes they did, his various holdings did business with them or their husbands and fathers and brothers. Sure they weren't as classy as the old-world wealthy, the true elite of this small country, but they were nothing to sneeze at.

He'd joined an etiquette class after his first million back when Sand Hill Road was the whole of Silicon Valley. He could use the right dessert fork when required. So it couldn't be the setting or the people he was mingling with.

After all, let's not forget the real reason he was here tonight. *Because no one else would have him.*

True to her chilly word, Aster had somehow managed to subtly but finally close the many, *many* doors previously opened to him.

His line of credit at the Bank of Singapore was frozen today as a surprise audit was being conducted on select clients. The last three properties his executive team had tried to buy for the as-yet unspecified campus had mysteriously become unavailable.

Not to mention, the dinner incident.

"Hey Drake," someone slurred next to him. "I heard you've been shit-canned from having dinner with the PM because the man was dining with old family friends."

Drake smiled tightly and murmured some nonsense. Although the man wasn't wrong. A message had been sent. Drake Fallahil was a guest and an unwelcome one, regardless of the dollars he was pouring into the economy.

At first it had been mildly amusing because he loved playing against a worthy adversary. Aster Chan was proving to be one hell of an adversary.

The bank audit would take a few weeks to untangle. His ego and portfolio could take all the hits she wanted to mete out. Missing dinner with the PM was a blow he had to live with.

Aster's broken heart was worth all this personal humiliation.

But then, she'd fucked with his people.

And that was a slight.

It wasn't unforgivable, yet, because the woman had also kept her word, literally, and sent him a fucking agreement through her lawyers laying down the terms of their situation clearly.

Marry her and be feted as the new king of one of the wealthiest nations.

Marry anyone else and still stay.

Or fuck the fuck off.

He'd not signed that travesty of a document because it was childish and ludicrous. He'd simply said yes the other night because it was the fastest way to make her leave.

But he'd sent her a crate of champagne as a touché along with his refusal note.

She'd sent him a video of pouring twenty-four bottles of 2000 Kristal down the toilet.

In hindsight, maybe he should have just said no to her.

But, then again, all the fighting, all the claim-staking was manna for him. He lived to box his way out of a corner, especially when the punches kept coming. He was *good* at it.

So, why was he bored?

Drake allowed his eyes to rove idly around the room. He could not honestly answer the question.

~ ~ ~ ~ ~

"Fallahil." Jay Runwal, one of the hosts and a prospective business partner, gave him a shit-eating grin. He held an enormous bottle of *Moet en Chandon* in one hand. "So glad you could make it."

Drake raised his half-empty martini glass. "Me too. This hits the spot, Runwal."

Two hangers-on from Runwal's entourage clung to him. He was a tall, broad-shouldered man with a fit physique and impeccable taste in clothing. A mirror of his brother, Ajay. Except, where Jay Runwal had inky black hair, Ajay had a streak of shocking white across his temple.

Jay handed the huge bottle to one of his people and pumped Drake's hand with the classic shill gesture, holding his elbow loosely while shaking his hand with the other. His eyes were friendly, easy-going.

Innately untrustworthy.

"So, have you had a chance to think about my proposal?"

The music was so loud, it should have shattered the glass walls. But they still held.

Drake shook his head. Pointed at his ear and shook his head again.

Jay flicked off his entourage and leaned in close to Drake to speak to him quietly. "Has your team had a chance to look at what Runwal Properties could offer you and your holdings?"

Drake gave him a small smile. "I believe they have. Yes."

The truth was, he was the team first. There wasn't a single piece of important legislation – financial, legal or otherwise – that he did not see at least once before having his people take care of it.

It was the best piece of advice his mentor had ever given him. *Treat your business like it's yours and it will be.*

"And?" Jay asked casually. "What do you think?"

"You know what I think?" Drake said slowly.

"Yes?" Jay smiled expansively, revealing shockingly white teeth against nut brown skin.

"How did you get those glass walls reinforced against the pandemonium playing here?" Drake pointed at the walls rising against the edge of the city, like they were suspended in an invisible bubble. "Was it some special form of silica concentrate still in prototype somewhere, or is there a company I can buy a stake in?"

Jay blinked. "I don't understand. "What do you mean?"

"What he means, dear brother." A man dressed in a crisp cream suit with a shock of white hair across his temple appeared next to Jay.

Ajay Runwal smiled at his brother and draped a heavy hand over his shoulder. "Is that tonight is for revelry. Business can wait till the week begins."

This man was dangerous, Drake figured instinctively. Because he understood what Drake wasn't saying. And Drake wasn't easily readable.

"I was talking business, Ajay." Drake shook hands with him. "But it wasn't the one your brother wanted to discuss."

"Aah. The walls." Ajay flicked a glance around the room. Taking it in, surveying it really. "I'll have someone send you the information about our company." Ajay smiled, tightly. "After all, we'd love to take your money one way or another."

"Indeed." Drake nodded slowly, as he finished the rest of his drink.

"Your glass is empty," Ajay observed needlessly. "Can't have that. What would you like to have? Whiskey? Something stronger." He pointed at the bar where a kindly lady was down to her panties and having tequila shots sucked off her concave belly. "Or something higher."

Ajay pointed at one of the servers, carrying little pills in silver goblets.

Drake's gut tightened as he saw a business acquaintance grab one goblet and pour its contents down the throat of his date. He'd squeezed her boob out of the tight pink dress she wore and was fondling it with impunity.

The woman's eyes turned glassy, her face went slack as the drugs hit her system.

All night long, he'd seen various versions of these dates being undressed and drugged and more in little corners, right out in the middle of the so-called dance floor.

Unfortunately, even looking at all of the nudity bared for him he was unmoved. Completely bored out of his 140 IQ brain.

"You want that, huh?" Ajay asked ruminatively. "Can't blame you. She's fucking hot."

He mistook Drake's interest for desire and Drake stiffened. He even opened his mouth to disabuse him of the notion when his interest was snagged.

Caught.

Riveted.

One of the women, the 'dates' the hosts had so helpfully procured for the night was sliding out of the giant party floor. She stuck to the edges of the glass wall till it merged with the wood paneling, giving access to the other rooms and areas of the penthouse.

She was a tiny thing in pointy shoes, encased in sheer black stockings.

The spit dried up in Drake's mouth at the sudden and explicit image he had of kneeling down and rolling them down her legs.

Her dark hair was artfully messed up to fall on her shoulders and her all-black outfit stood out against the hot colors and splashy choices of the other guests.

But it wasn't her clothes or the line of her legs, silkily visible halfway across this great expanse of a room that riveted him.

It was the expression on her face.

Illuminated, as if a spotlight had been cast on her, especially for him. Because no one else, not the people snorting and drinking and injecting or screwing each other or the helpful but invisible wait staff, was watching her. They were all focused on each other.

And in a sea of people who were intent on numbing themselves, this woman seemed out of place with how fragile and alive she was.

Something stirred in him at the expression on her half-hidden face.

It was unmitigated rage mingled with stark, naked fear.

She squeezed against the wall, almost becoming one with it. Then slipped into an inner recess which was all black, disappearing from view like a wraith.

"Drake?" Ajay prompted him, breaking into his thoughts. "Who do you want?"

Her, his mind responded instantly. Very much present, un-bored.

"Another drink," Drake murmured. "I think." He gave the hosts a wide smile fanning out every single one of his laugh lines. "This is an amazing party, guys. Let's talk business Monday."

He raised his empty glass on a toast and walked away to investigate the only thing of interest to him in the party from hell.

FOUR

The inside of the Runwals' home was as expansive as the outside had been.

An hour of mingling with the guests and Anya was breathless. Giddy and a little sick. From the amount of illegal substances, food, and alcohol she'd seen so casually consumed. From the slick sounds of voracious sexual appetites being fulfilled with no thought to privacy or decorum – if everyone involved was high as a fucking kite.

Then, there were the damn glass walls...sheer and death-defying.

She'd known they would be there, when she'd tracked the Runwals' socials and familiarized herself with their lifestyle. This apartment.

The floor plan was fairly simple and open in layout. The kitchen and dining area were separate from the living section by a line of potted plants, about ten feet high. And the lights and furnishings changed from stark, serious wood to soft, white wicker and marble. Next to the kitchen was a solid wall which gave the illusion of this being all the space there was in the apartment.

But, she knew, there was a secret paneled door on the wooden wall. Right next to the Frida Kahlo original hanging square in the middle.

Her destination lay beyond it, in the inner passages of this godforsaken house.

But right now, she had to deal with what was in front of her. The people and the walls. Three of the four-walled apartment were covered by the glass. And people were pressed up against each other, inch for inch across all three walls.

But knowing about the glass walls and seeing them, being encased inside them were two different things. Not to mention being trapped with people who'd left their common sense on the elevator ride over to this den of iniquity.

She'd endured ass grabs and waist squeezes from both men and women, some of them had even guest lectured at NUS for one of her business admin classes. Stockbrokers and property developers and young tech moguls mingling with the truly filthy rich of the city.

If she allowed herself to think about it, she'd spit in the faces of these bastards who so casually used the labor, dignity, and knowledge of those they considered lesser than them with no regrets at all.

Most of all, *Ajay Runwal.*

"Come." A drunk Elon Musk-type in jeans and cowboy shirt (with fringes on the side) slurred against Anya's neck. "Come with me."

She draped a hand over the man's shoulder. He smelled of sweaty beer and his own scent, an expensive Italian brand with shower and soap. Good-looking enough, she supposed.

At least, unlike Tonya's date, he had a full head of hair. And he wasn't biting at her neck like she was a tasty tidbit brought here for his consumption.

"Yes." She leaned into the Cowboy. "Okay."

He grabbed her waist and fingered her hair, it had come down from the messy updo she'd tried to style it in in order to look older and sophisticated. Now she just had a lot of nape sweat and her curls were unraveling.

"Sexy," he commented.

"Thank you." She meant it.

"You're sexy too." The man's erection poked at her thigh. It wasn't impressive but she didn't hold it against him. At least, he was still talking to her instead of…well other things. "Come."

The cowboy's eyes roved down her dress. It was a basic little black dress with puffy sleeves and a boat neckline, cut short at the hem, so it hit her just above mid-thigh. She'd worn the fishnet stockings to dress it up a little. But, in this atmosphere, it looked like everything else – seductive and up for sale.

"Anika."

Her name was pinned on her chest, like all the other girls from the Fuck Bus. Those who still managed to keep their clothes on, that is.

She nodded. "That's my name."

Anya snagged a glass of something amber from a passing tray and tossed half of it back. She took a deep breath and found the cowboy's eyes transfixed on her chest. The damn dress was a size too tight and when she took deep breaths her boobs kind of…spilled out a little.

The cowboy licked his lips.

Anya's stomach tightened in revulsion. She couldn't believe she would have to let this man touch her. Do more if there was no other way out. *FUCK.*

The man leaned in and kissed her neck. Well, he swabbed his tongue all over the side of her neck, leaving it wet and glistening. His oily-black eyes gleamed with instant lust and desire, just not desire for her.

The desire to *have* her.

She'd seen it so many times, in so many different places it left her cold and unmoved. Unbearably alone.

He ran a thick finger down her neck. "That's a neck made for a pearl necklace. Isn't it?"

Anya's stomach dropped out. She knew he wasn't talking about actual jewelry. Her skin crawled. She fisted her hand against her side, resisting the urge to push him away. Her head reeled from trying to stay upright in the crush of bodies on the party floor.

"Listen…"

The speakers blew out a popular dance number then. Anya could have cried in gratitude and relief.

She grabbed the man's hands and placed them both around her waist. Bass thumped the glass walls but didn't shatter them. Panic and disgust and sheer terror snaked their way inside Anya's body, hardening her spine but weakening her knees.

She ground against her 'date' for the evening.

"I love this song." Anya blew into his ears, stretching on her toes since she was still a few inches short on heels. "Don't you?"

The cowboy pushed his arousal into her stomach but kept time with the beat. "Fuck, yeah."

~ ~ ~ ~ ~ ~

Saved by the fucking beat, Anya thought. She'd avoided imminent disaster for the moment and the humiliation sure to follow if the man tried something with her.

She couldn't risk having her cover blown and a chance to do what she'd promised to do tonight, but having to endure anymore of any of these loathsome and vile people's attentions was a line she wasn't sure she could cross.

The dance ended with Anya encouraging the cowboy to down a goblet full of pills.

Her own pill, the one she'd tucked under her tongue and discarded the second she'd exited the elevator had left her with a sour and slightly metallic taste. She was afraid to think too deeply in case that caused a hit to her system and dopamine or other hormones were released by the drug.

The cowboy's eyes rolled back when he chased the pills with champagne straight from the bottle.

Anya turned around, jigging in place and spotted Ajay. He was unmistakable in his cream linen summer suit, jacket open. And the shock of white hair at his temples.

Rumor had it, he'd deliberately cultivated those greys to distinguish himself from his identical but somehow more handsome brother, Jay.

She had little doubt believing Ajay was capable of something so small and petty.

Her spine stiffened because Ajay's beetle-black eyes swept over every guest in this corner of the floor. Even her. They were idle but sharp nevertheless. Like the beacon light of a lighthouse sweeping over choppy waters.

Anya almost held her breath as Ajay's gaze went past her, not recognizing her. Or even knowing she was here.

But he didn't know her. Not as Anya or anything else. She was of no interest to him. Because she wasn't clever and malleable.

She did not have self-destructive tendencies or a propensity to fly close to the sun in the hopes of getting a sunburn.

She was *normal.*

Anya turned to the cowboy, renewed determination giving her soft brown eyes a hectic glitter. Even the color was high on her bronzed cheeks, artfully made up by one of her classmates at uni.

"Want to get out of here?"

The cowboy's eyes focused blearily on her. Whatever he'd ingested had kicked in and his pupils were blown. He nodded, slowly as if with great effort.

"Yes," he rumbled.

Anya looked at the wall, opposite to her. She was about thirty feet from the Kahlo painting, and if she tilted her head to the side and blurred her eyes a little, she could almost feel that feminist icon smiling at her, beckoning her inside.

So, the Runwals could have their comeuppance, at long last.

She draped the cowboy's arms around her waist, winding her own around his sweaty and beefy neck.

Any pushed him, bit by bit, towards her goal. The wooden paneled wall. The cowboy's hands cupped her butt and squeezed and she felt bile rise up her throat. She took a deep breath trying to control it and the man grinned, thoroughly bombed out of his head.

She ardently wished he'd pass out soon so she wouldn't have to use the chloroform-soaked tissue she'd smuggled in an inner lining of the dress.

Along with that other thing.

"Give me a kiss, baby." The cowboy leaned in close, puckering his lips in anticipation of her mouth.

They were almost there, almost, the Kahlo self-portrait brilliantly lit from the inside.

Anya gave Frida an apologetic look and quickly pecked the cowboy on the lips. Her own lips were cold and small, undesirable.

He smelled of liquor and whatever horrible thing he'd downed before the champagne. He smelled weak and worthless.

It seemed to satisfy his need and he placed his considerably heavy head on Anya's shoulder. She was ten feet from the Kahlo painting.

He burped, a quiet little sound and slunk on her. Transferring his weight on her.

All around them, people partied. Oblivious to the cowboy's almost passing out.

Anya almost staggered against two hundred pounds of drunk male. She maneuvered so he was to the side and sort of dragged-walked him to the wall. It was hot, sweaty work and more of her hair came down, some of her makeup streaked away from her cheeks and chin too, to reveal the smooth unblemished skin her mother was so proud of.

The writhing crowd didn't part but they didn't get in her way either, so she was able to make her way unnoticed to where she wanted to go.

The Kahlo painting.

The cowboy burped again. And gave a little snore to boot.

She propped him against a leather ottoman –like thing, a little to the left of the painting and kissed him on the cheek. So, onlookers would remember she'd taken care of him.

Then the crowd closed around the man and Anya melted next to the wall.

~ ~ ~ ~ ~ ~

She kept her gaze straight and sure, trying to keep Runwal in sight, as she inched to the painting.

He was talking to his brother, who held an unholy large bottle of champagne in his hands.

Anya gulped a hot breath down as sick nerves and dazzling adrenaline twisted inside her. Giving her the courage to move a few inches at a time, all the while keeping her enemy in sight.

Her spine stiffened, almost cracking in two as she caught sight of the person, man, the Runwal brothers were talking to.

He wore a smoothly tailored suit with a black shirt, black and unforgiving like the Devil. And he had burnished hair that gleamed even under the low lights of the party room. He was taller than the Runwal brothers, by a good two inches.

But that wasn't what made her breath catch. Her spine arch in sheer fright.

It was the fact that in the mass of two hundred people, all of whom were uncontrolled and wild and uninhibited, this man seemed to stand still. He was comfortable in his skin, as he gestured with his martini glass. Unbothered by whatever was happening around him. No reaction at all.

Like a black hole had been created by his very presence and all of the depravity and insanity flowed into him but didn't touch him; he stood apart from it all.

And he was looking right back at her. His face in shadow but backlit like he was the star of his own private show in this nightmare.

His eyes arcing bright blue light, *right at her.*

Fear – of the man's brilliant gaze, of the Runwals discovering her location, of what she was attempting to do – gave her momentum.

She notched her chin up just an inch higher.

Fuck him. Whoever he was. He was here enjoying these fiends' hospitality, eating their food and drinking their expensive liquor and whatever else they'd give him. That made him a monster by association.

She was here to save her family. To make things right for her mother. She wasn't going to allow anyone to fuck up her mission.

Anya's fingers found and depressed the small button she'd been searching for the last five seconds of staring at the black hole man. She felt the small whoosh of air as the concealed door slid open.

Anya slipped in. Wanting to keep her gaze on the man who was her enemy. But the truth was, she was looking at the other man.

The one whose eyes were so blue they looked like the sky.

She melted into the passage inside, and took a deep breath. It was clear…cool. Blessedly normal. The air inside cold and temperature-controlled. Free of the miasma of fluids – human and otherwise – in the other room.

The door slid shut behind her.

Anya looked up at the camera installed on the corridor. Slid out of the first layer of her dress – it stretched – and tossed it on the camera.

Then she grabbed her shoes, held them close to her chest and started running.

<div style="text-align: center;">~~~~~</div>

The soft carpeting, faux plush if she wasn't mistaken, muffled the signs of her slapping feet as she sprinted down the long and well-lit passageway. Thankfully, there were no more cameras in this part of the house.

She came to another door. This one unlocked the old-fashioned way, with a handle, and came to a proper apartment. It was designed in navy and cream. Like a mirror of the other apartment, except everything was done up on the other side…and there were no glass walls.

It was a regular apartment, with the appropriate amount of privacy. It even had winding stairs leading down to the other floors that made up the brothers' home.

She took the stairs on her immediate right. Thundering down, while her heart tried to burst out of her chest. Her breathing was so loud she felt like she was hyperventilating and, every few seconds, she checked the lined pocket of the flimsy slip she wore under the dress.

The little bulge there reassured her as much as the sound of utter and blissful silence. It was as if the party was happening on another planet, and this whole space was soundproofed to within an inch of the heated flooring.

She went down, two, three flights of stairs. And came upon a sterile black and grey space - the second office where Ajay kept a set of servers so he was never out of touch with work. A pair of cameras were mounted on the entrance to the server room and the office.

She quickly unrolled her stockings and threw each one on the cameras.

Because Runwal was such a paranoid bastard, he'd been careful to place no cameras *inside* the server room.

Of course, he had to be. Given how he and his family had made their millions in the first place. They'd want no evidence – video or otherwise – of their nefarious work ethics.

This was going to be his downfall.

The watch on her secret phone beeped.

She had three minutes max to do what needed doing before all hell broke less.

The fifty by fifty feet room was freezing cold, because the servers – freestanding structures encased in fire and shatter proof glass – blinked and worked twenty-four/seven.

Anya's nipples beaded against the satin slip she wore. She rubbed her elbows roughly, trying to dispel the goose bumps rising all over her body. She tied her hair up in a haphazard bun, but some of it slid down when she bent down at the lone table in the room.

She patted at the desk, searching desperately. "Come on. Come on. Open up."

As if her command was answered, the plain wooden table split into two and a computer rose from the inside. It booted up in three seconds while the mouse and keyboard slid up.

Her phone beeped a two minute warning.

The room was freezing cold and Anya wiped sweat off her forehead. The desktop screensaver showed her files and folders, clustered against each other. The naming system was jumbled, intentionally, no doubt. And it looked quite ugly, in fact.

Not the smooth and elegant system of one of the better real estate developers in the city.

But Anya knew it was a façade. Ishqi had told her so. It was yet another safeguard Runwal had created in case someone came close to hacking his system.

Somewhere in this mess and jumble were the files that proved her sister had indeed worked with Runwal on a black hat job – hacking – to undercut their competitors on an important government infrastructure project tender.

Except, Runwal had screwed up phenomenally. Or he'd known how to tie up loose ends.

Now, Ishqi was rotting in jail for the last three months because it had come down to her word against Runwal's. No proof.

Anya needed to stick the little thumb drive she'd carefully smuggled into this place under her ridiculous party get up. It would bypass all of Runwal's firewalls and tripwires, neatly replicate his user signature and copy everything on the damn servers. The thumb drive had the memory capacity of a large power station – somewhere north of a thousand terra bytes.

Thousand and twenty four TB, Anya. Ishqi's husky and playful voice corrected her.

Then, all Anya would exit through one of the lower floors, leaving behind evidence of a drunk and stoned-out party girl. And no one would be the wiser.

She fingered the tiny device that was going to save her sister, clear her name and bring her back home so mama would have the damn operation that would save her knees!

Her phone beeped a ninety second warning.

Anya removed the thumb drive, unzipping most of her slip in the process so it gaped open at the midriff and exposed her right breast to the chilly HVAC unit working overtime here.

She ignored the freezing of her hands and her skin and was about to stick the USB drive into the computer monitor when someone coughed.

Anya froze.

"I wouldn't do that if I were you." That voice…it was quietly amused, very contained. Almost inaudible.

"What?" She husked out.

Everything in her clenched tight in sheer terror. FUCK. She'd been so close. *SO CLOSE.* She couldn't just…

Anya touched the monitor.

An ear-splitting blast hit her ears. Actual sirens burst open from the four corners of the ceilings.

Anya looked back at the intruder in alarm. Understanding the supreme irony of considering this person an intruder while she was one too.

The black hole man nodded at the monitor, where she was still touching it. "That."

Anya stared, helpless, terrified, *frozen* at the man who seemed to be a whole island of calm….no…not calm, of stillness. Utter and complete stillness. While the world went to hell around her and she knew, without a doubt, that her fate would be worse than what happened to Ishqi.

She, Anya figured, was unequivocally and completely fucked.

FIVE

Drake's first mentor was a man named Daiquiri, like the cocktail, for the cocktails he loved drinking more than anything in the whole world. He'd met Daiquiri during his first off-shore oil rig gig, where he'd been given the shittiest of jobs, shoveling the crude in boiling temperatures, among other things.

Daiquiri was a big, buff dude who wore overalls and a red bandana like a badge of freaking pride. Drake had found him to be always cheerful while working alongside him. Later on, Drake figured it was because he was cheerfully drunk most of the time.

But, Daiquiri was a rich motherfucker who could beat anyone at cards.

For the first two months, Daiquiri had sat at the games table every night and cleaned out half the deck's pay before they earned it. Drake included.

Then, for some reason that Drake never understood even now, almost two decades later, the man had decided to take Drake under his cheerful wing.

And thus Drake's education in the fine art of fleecing money from people had begun. It was called Texas Hold

'Em Poker but Daiquiri laughingly told Drake it was about taking money from people who were willing to part with it.

And he gave Drake the most important advice he'd ever receive in his whole life.

You want to know how to win at three-card Monte, Drakey-boy? Don't play.

The lesson here was, of course, ridiculously simple. Never play for more than you can afford to lose. But Drake had understood what the man meant.

Never assume you'll win everything. Always assume you'll lose something. And so spot the pattern that will help you lose less of that something and win more of everything.

But, Daiquiri's other pertinent advice was what Drake had tattooed in his brain.

Find the anomaly. The one thing that doesn't belong in the room, the situation, the game… in your opponent. Use it to your advantage before anyone else.

In poker, this had meant identifying the 'tells' of the players, by simply studying their posture when they played, but also by paying *attention* when they weren't playing.

If a player heard good news from home, he was in a looser frame of mind. He felt lucky and, thus, was easier to bluff against. A man who'd had a shitty day was harder to bet against.

The trick was in knowing which was which.

In venture capital fueled by future commodities investments, this had meant a million different things – such as reading newspapers from seventeen different markets, talking to people from all walks of life so he understood the pain points of the consumers and could invest in those companies – startups – providing solutions to these problems. It had meant putting together delicate deals that cost millions and was nothing more than pure speculation in the worth and success of a piece of technical innovation, thousands of lines of code.

Nine times out of ten, he'd picked out the thing no one was seeing and made bank when the world caught up to his way of thinking.

Tonight, it simply meant following an intriguing beauty down a hidden hallway.

Drake still felt the same rush of adrenalin and pure energy he got when he was structuring a VC deal that could fall apart with one whiff of negative publicity. When he'd sat at the poker table and won a royal flush against Daiquiri all those years ago.

He reached the Frida Kahlo painting, barely paying mind to the people gyrating around him. He hoped to God, the Runwals were busy elsewhere, although he was reasonably sure Ajay Runwal was a sharp shooter.

Drake nodded vacantly at a couple nearby. Where the chairman of one of the premier investment firms in Hong Kong was 'dancing' with a woman not his wife.

His fingers searched for a catch under the painting and found a depression. He pressed on it and the hideaway door opened again.

He slipped in before it was open fully and hit the button to shut it before his absence could be noticed.

Then, out of habit, he looked up at the raised ceiling with the CCTV cam and broke into a full-out grin.

The girl was smart. Crazy smart. She'd covered the camera with something black and flimsy.

He leaned one lazy arm up and brought the thing down. The camera was visible again.

For added effect, Drake gave a broad grin at the camera and leisurely strolled on.

He entered the other penthouse; it was empty of occupants. But there were stairs leading up and down. Following instinct and a vague knowledge of the Runwals' floor plan, he took the steps leading down, three at a time.

When he arrived at the floor with a large reinforced door marked SERVER ROOM in English and Malay, he knew he'd hit jackpot.

Then, there were the two slinky underthings, black fishnets, draped haphazardly over the two outward facing cameras.

For a brief, insanely hot second he entertained the thought of slipping inside and finding this beauty completely naked. But it was only for a second.

No, if she'd covered all the cameras, knowing security would be alerted sooner rather than later, she was here for a purpose. A mission.

It would be Drake's profound pleasure to find out what she wanted in the bowels of the Runwals' server room.

He lightly toed the door open – Runwal had overestimated his internal alarm system and was now paying for it – and entered the room.

It was bitching cold. Especially after the cloistering heat from Bacchanalia.

It took a few seconds for his eyes to adjust to the low-heat skim lights. To make out the slim figure of the woman as she bent over the single computer terminal in the whole room. Right next to the bank of free-standing server modules in the middle of the room.

Her legs were toned and ridiculously sexy, now that she was barefoot. And the line of her shoulders in the slip dress she wore was outrageously tempting.

Drake was about to step farther into the room when he caught the faintest glimmer of red and green around the computer monitor.

He narrowed his eyes, unsure of his eyesight. Then it happened again and he saw it.

A tiny motion-sensor field constructed around the monitor. Ready to trip and sound the alarm when anyone other than approved personnel touched the computer.

So, he coughed. Rather loudly.

The woman froze.

He felt the pull of her action in his belly.

"I wouldn't do that if I were you," he said pleasantly. Taking care to not move an inch in either direction.

The woman whipped her slender neck and speared him with a look. It was stunned, accusing…apprehensive. His belly tightened as he deciphered each individual feeling she telegraphed so clearly.

Her dark eyes were so expressive he almost felt bad for her. Almost.

"What?" Her voice was low. Defiant.

Something beeped on the woman.

She turned around and touched the monitor, her fingers passing through the sensor field. Triggering the alarm.

Drake kept his wince at the god-awful racket in as manfully as he could.

"That," he said grimly. He nodded at where her hand was still inside the sensor field.

The woman's expression changed to utter horror as she realized the implications of what had just occurred.

Then, something strange happened.

~ ~ ~ ~ ~ ~

Her spine snapped straight, as if she'd been yanked upward by a chain. Her expression went glass-smooth.

Unreadable. It was an impressive about-face if he hadn't seen her fingers clench at the side of the flimsy piece of clothing she wore.

"I…"

Drake's bat-sensitive ears caught the sound of pounding feet coming down the stairs. He gripped the dress and stockings he held and stuffed them into his pants pockets, crossing the room in three swift strides.

The woman's eyes widened before she realized his intent.

He reached her, grabbing her waist without so much as a word and clutched her closer to him. Her body was cold to the touch, where he touched her front to back. Her nails dug into his forearm where he held her.

They looked at each other breathlessly for a long moment.

Her eyes were dark brown, almost hazel, he thought irrelevantly.

And they were furious instead of terrified.

Her red-slick lips parted and he had the distinct notion she was going to scream. Which was stupid and brave. But nothing about this woman was vaguely normal.

He dipped his head closer to her, his belly clenched to the point of pain at proximity with her. Her scent was subtle, some kind of a flowery fragrance under the more obvious scents from the party – liquor, illegal substances, and designer perfumes. Her skin flushed golden as he breathed on her.

"Just go with me, okay?" he instructed her. Holding her closer when she took a surprised breath.

The strap of her silky slip slid down revealing the crest of one rounded breast gaping open at one side, the nipple pointing up, no doubt due to the freezing air.

Drake was appalled because he had such an explicit vision of whipping her about, bending down and tonguing that point. He was afraid he'd already done it.

But, then his famed control brought him back from the edge.

"What's happening?" she muttered, twisting against him.

"Don't move."

Security entered the room in a rush but Drake only had eyes for the woman in his arms.

He laid one hand on the open side of her slip, his cold fingers searching for the inside zipper. He found it and drew it up, slowly, excruciatingly. Keeping his lips right near hers so it looked to anyone that they were enjoying a deeply passionate embrace.

"The guards are here. I'm going to tell them you're with me. Don't contradict me. Okay?"

His finger brushed the curve of her breast and he willed his blood to cool down. This was not the moment to get aroused. His control held and he was able to finish zipping her up, moving up to cup her shoulders.

The guards were shouting in Malay and English.

But their sounds were muffled. As if he was enclosed in a bubble with this woman, and water lapped at the edges of the bubble.

She continued looking up at him, no expression on her half-lit face. But her skin spoke to him. Flushed, when the temperature was a cool twelve degrees. Her fingers moved jerkily against his thigh, the hard band of his hand on her waist. Her chest took sharp breaths, as if there was jagged glass inside her.

Most of all, he could hear the thump-thump of her heart beat in a furious wild rhythm.

Or maybe that was him with his heart and pulse out of all control.

The thought shocked him enough to burst his bubble.

The sounds and people in the periphery of his consciousness rushed to the forefront.

He half-turned his head and saw five Schmeissers pointed at his face.

~ ~ ~ ~ ~ ~

The woman sucked in a panicked breath. He gave her warm shoulder what he hoped was a reassuring squeeze.

"I apologize," he said in a slightly exaggerated American drawl. "My date and I…" He patted at the woman's naked skin again. "We were looking for somewhere private to…conclude our evening."

He brushed his lips over her neck. She dug one fingernail into his hand. Almost penetrating his suit.

"And you thought the server room was the best option?" One of the guards demanded.

The guns did not waver.

Drake shrugged. "I didn't know what it was called, man. The door was open, the room was empty. And there was a handy horizontal surface." He deliberately waved a hand in the direction of the sensor field, setting the alarm off again.

"Ouch. That hurts."

He dipped his lips close to her neck again and muttered, "Smile. Like you mean it."

The woman licked her lips and a shaft of desire went through him like his control meant nothing.

Then she spoke in softly-accented Malay. Patting Drake's arm and pointing at the door and her dress hanging from his pocket. She finished with a shy smile tilting her face up at him.

"The girl says you made her run. Is that true?" The guard demanded of Drake.

Drake's eyes telegraphed chagrin and respect. *Touche,* he thought.

"Yeah," he said blithely. "I was bored in there, you know." He raised the woman's hand and kissed the cold tips. "She's the most interesting diversion I've had in a long time."

Her eyes shuttered even more but she played her part. She leaned close to him. "I'm so glad to be here."

The guards muttered something. Then one of them held one hand up to his earpiece. "That's Ajay sir. Asking us about the disturbance."

"Cool. Let's call him," Drake agreed with equanimity.

The woman's spine stiffened again and she glared at him. Furious and panicked.

But, he knew people, security guards. So he knew, such breaches were serious business for security guards.

They'd hardly want their failure advertised to their employers.

"Tell you what, gentlemen?" He dug into his inner coat pocket and came up with a wad of dollars. US. "Why don't you consider this a thank you for your kindly services tonight and let me and my…" He gave the girl a tender but smoldering hot grin.

And he actually meant it. "Date go find that horizontal surface."

The guards looked at him, at his guileless grin, and the wad of cash he held, a cool twenty thousand dollars, when the difference was split.

He could actually see the thought process as it formed step-by-step in their brains. The moment when they reached the conclusion he wanted them to.

The only one that worked for him.

The lead guard, the one who'd asked all the questions, reached out and took the money from Drake's outstretched hand. Gingerly.

"Get out. And go back to the party, lah," one of the other guards suggested.

"Thanks, man. We will."

Drake swept one hand in front of the woman; who picked up her shoes with a breathless smile. She clutched them to her chest and preceded him out the server room.

Two of the guards followed them back up the stairs and to the upper floors. When they came to the empty penthouse, Drake asked them pleasantly, "Any rooms available here?" He wiggled his eyebrows. "You know, private ones?"

The two guards looked at each other. Then expectantly at him.

He reached into his coat and removed another wad. The woman's eyes narrowed, he could feel it happen muscle by muscle.

One guard reached out and took the money while the other one reached into his coat pocket and extracted a keycard, like those found in hotels. He swiped it against the nearest wall and a door opened about thirty feet ahead in the plush carpeted hallway.

Drake grinned. Another wide, aw shucks thank you so much grin. "Thank you, gentlemen. You've contributed significantly to my good mood tonight."

They nodded and clanked up the stairs, their guns held loosely but competently.

The woman sucked in another rabbit-like breath while Drake yanked her forward, gently but inexorably toward the door.

The woman started struggling. "Let me go."

"Let me *go,* you fiend."

He reached the door and shoved her through it shutting it behind them while she tried to kick him. He simply used his superior strength to clamp her mouth shut while her hot breath feathered against his cold palm and her eyes spit holy fire at him.

It was amusing and, yes, arousing. He didn't have time for either.

"I just saved your ass from being thrown into jail or worse, sweetheart," he began grimly. "The least you can do is thank me before screaming the place down."

She took another breath.

He pulled her dress from his pocket. Held it between them.

"Wear it," he suggested. "Then we talk. Okay?"

SIX

Anya reeled. Her thoughts were in complete chaos and disarray, with panic leading the charge. When she'd first heard the alarms, all of her brain had shut down until only the basest, most animal part of her mind remained.

That part wanted to survive. At any cost.

It had allowed the strangely familiar and scarily hot man to come in and take charge. *Touch* her so intimately, as if they belonged together. That part clamped the rational part of her mind down in a vise so tight she could only breathe in shallow gasps.

It came out to play to talk, no, coo softly at the guards with the scary guns.

She'd recognized them instantly. Their bearing screamed military, with the buzz cuts and the peculiar way they held their shoulders so tightly straight.

Her insides quivered while the scary hot man bribed the skeptical guards with money. Lots of money. Too much money. She'd helped him along, allowing him to touch and feather a kiss on her neck.

A searing burn suffusing her skin when he did so. A touch she wouldn't forget, *ever.*

Then, mercifully they were allowed to leave the server room and proceed up the stairs, alive. In one piece. And without Ajay Runwal's knowledge.

She couldn't allow herself to feel too disappointed at having left her mission incomplete, considering the alternative. Her relief at having made it out was too real.

It was the only reason she didn't pay attention when her mysterious rescuer talked pleasantly with the guards. She only snapped out of her reverie when more money exchanged hands and the man gave the guards an affable smile.

The guard swiped a card on an invisible card reader and a door opened farther down the hallway.

Alarm shot through her when the man dragged her, none too gently, down the hallway while the guards disappeared.

That's when Anya realized one crucial thing.

This man was a bigger threat than Runwal and his security guards.

For one thing, despite the deceptive cut of his fine suit, he was solidly built. She'd felt the hard lines of his arms and hand as he held her indecently close back in the server room.

Secondly, he was taller than her, topping her by more than half a feet. So he had longer legs, even though she'd raced track during high school.

He shoved her into the room before she could voice a real protest.

Then her common sense and vocal chords kicked in. She'd wanted to scream, claw at his ridiculously pretty face – what she could see of it.

"Let me go," she gritted out, as ungodly visions of this man doing what he wanted with her filled her head with…panic…yes, it was enraged panic.

What else could it be?

The skin at the side of her breast throbbed as if he'd touched her all over again. Anya felt betrayed by her own body.

"Let me *go,* you fiend."

He said something she didn't hear exactly with all the blood rushing into her. Adrenalin kicked in and gave her fight instincts.

The man hauled her away from the door with ease. The force field of his eyes finally tore through her adrenalin, leaving her naked and shivering.

Inside and out.

He thrust her dress at her. "Wear it and we talk. Okay?"

~ ~ ~ ~ ~

Since it was the lesser of two evils, she took the dress from him with an angry oath. She squeezed into it with economical movements, aware of his silent scrutiny. For good measure, she even turned her back on him. A supremely bad idea.

During the time, he snapped on a tiny light that hid more than highlighted him.

Never turn your back on an assailant, Anya! Master Lam, her self-defense instructor, boomed in her ear.

When she turned around, settling her escaped hair around her shoulders, she bumped into *him.*

He didn't loom…he had no need to. He was just there. Present. Taking up room around her, until it felt as if he was the source of all energy.

Anya was forced to tilt her chin and look up at him, given their height differences. Her breath escaped through her parted lips when their gazes collided.

His eyes were a pure endless blue, with no hint of black or grey.

It was disturbing. Hypnotic. *Known.*

Anya sucked in yet another shocked breath. "You're DRAKE Fallahil." She spoke in Malay, one of Singapore's many dialects.

The knowledge of that name, of what it stood for… who he *was,* dropped into her consciousness with all the devastation of a bomb. Instant and annihilating.

The man, Drake Fallahil, actually took an imperceptible step back at her proclamation.

She knew it because the air cleared, just a smidge, and she could breathe again. She could put two thoughts together.

"You're Drake Fallahil," she said again.

This time in his language. English.

"I heard you the first time, you know," he said mildly.

His voice was soft, not exactly the deep baritone she thought all billionaires cultivated when the eighth zero appeared in their portfolios. But it wasn't weak. No, it was the opposite of weak. Like his presence.

It simply was unassailable fact.

Hearing it set off a tectonic shift off in her stomach, which swooped down to her knees.

Anya stumbled backward. One step, then two. All the starch seeped out of her. The backs of her knees bumped against something, the bed's counterpane. She sat down on it with a huge gusty sigh, still not really seeing him.

This made no sense. None of it.

"That makes two of us," Drake Fallahil said grimly.

Anya gave him a startled glance. She'd spoken out loud. Fuck.

Her luck was truly, spectacularly bad.

She'd been rescued by the one man rumored to be worse than all the other money men put together. The man without a conscience, or a heart. The man who made a habit of collecting debt and equity like other men collected useless memorabilia.

"You shouldn't have done that." She clenched her fingers together, as if it could keep her heart from leaping out of its chest. *As if it could save her now.*

"Done what? Rescue you?" Drake Fallahil cocked his head to one side and gold lights shone through his dark waves. Making the blue of his eyes stand out like freaking headlights.

Anya felt blinded. Stunned.

"Next time I won't bother. Shall I?"

She shook her head, it ached like a mother. She clutched at the edges of her temple and tried to make sense of what happened. *How* it happened. And how to get out of it.

Drake Fallahil's immaculate wingtips, came into her line of vision, lining up toe to toe against her own feet. She withdrew her feet, tucked them under knees.

"So, what *were* you doing in the Runwals' server room?"

She said nothing.

"Alright, let's try another question. Who sent you? Was it a rival developer? A little corporate espionage? The authorities? Trying to get a little sting op going?" He suggested outrageous things, one after the other.

Anya tried to keep the giggle in. It was incongruous, given the circumstances. But the idea of her being some kind of femme fatale spy was even more ludicrous.

The laugh burst out of her without volition. She covered her mouth with both hands, her shoulders shaking while she tried to stop laughing. A few seconds, the giggles turned into wheezes.

She still wouldn't, couldn't, look at him.

Drake Fallahil muttered an oath under his breath and sat down beside her.

She immediately tried to squeeze into a tinier ball, while the wheezing became short, gasping breaths. She couldn't get in enough air.

He put one hand over her skull, tunneling his long, warm fingers through her hair, disturbing the up-do even further. His pressure was inexorable. He pushed her skull down till it hung over her knees.

"Breathe," he advised. "Deep breaths."

She tried to give him an upside-down glance of indignation.

"You're having a panic attack. Reaction, most likely," he explained. "Breathe with your head between your knees. You should be fine."

Unbelievably, his instructions worked and, after five deep calming breaths, she could actually herself think.

Clearly.

Finally her brain began to wake up. Catch up to the predicament she found herself in. Assimilate the facts, as they were.

Fact one, she'd been rescued by one of the richest and most elusive men in the world. Fact two, he was hotter than any picture had ever done him justice. Fact three, he was rubbing her back right now, as if he really cared about her.

And, unforgivable fact four, her spine was moving against his touch. Like a feline receiving loving attention from someone important. As if she could *trust* him.

~~~~~

"What are you *doing?*" Anya hissed as she stood up, on uncertain legs.

He tugged her down with one flimsy touch, patted her shoulder again. "Take a moment. Catch your breath."

Anya shook her head but breathed deeply. Then she glanced at him. Drake Fallahil.

"You…I…What happened?" She demanded.

"Well, I bribed the Runwals' security to the tune of twenty-five thousand USD for you." He winked at her. "You can thank me now."

"I don't have that kind of money to repay you," she snapped out.

"I wasn't looking for that kind of thanks, sweetheart," he reassured her.
~~~~~

Anya stiffened. She slid a discreet inch away from him. Aware of the rest of the facts her brain had assimilated while she'd had her meltdown.

They were alone in an unmanned part of this penthouse suite. They were locked in together in what was certainly a bedroom. He was significantly larger than her in every way imaginable.

And…she swallowed as she took in his saturnine expression, he looked capable of many dark, unnamed sins.

"I wasn't looking for *that* kind of thanks, either. Jesus." Drake Fallahil rubbed a hand over his jaw. His bristle scraped over his palm, the sound loud in the still room.

"Then why did you follow me?" It was the most logical explanation of what happened. And it still made no sense.

Because for him to follow her, he had to have been watching her. And she'd been so sure, so *sure* she was nondescript. Undetected.

How could he have been watching her when she was no one?

"I told you. You were the most interesting diversion at that party. Of course, I followed you. Now." He raised both hands in an expansive gesture. "Are you going to tell me what you were doing, breaking into the Runwals' server room?"

For a single mad moment, she was tempted to tell him everything. Confide the mess her life had become. But only for a moment. Then sanity reasserted itself and she gave him a wary look.

"If I don't will you call the guards on me?"

"I went to a lot of trouble keeping the guards away from you," he replied slowly. "Why would I call them back?"

Because that's what men who are thwarted, do. Especially powerful men.

Anya shook her head again. "Then, no. I am not telling you a thing." She waited with suspended breath to see what he'd do next.

In her experience, thwarted men usually expressed their frustration. Took it out on the one thwarting them.

~ ~ ~ ~ ~

"Okay. I would like to know one thing, though."

"What?" She was still wary.

"How did you know where the cameras were going to be? And how many? I mean…" He gave her a slow-as-molasses smile. It began somewhere in his eyes and ended south of his lips. "What if there had been more than three cameras? What else were you prepared to throw at them?"

"That's a vile thing to ask." She clenched her fingers tight.

"It's a very practical thing to ask actually." Drake leaned back against the bed, his elbows supporting his considerable, legs spread wide. *Lounging.*

"Because, whoever gave you your intel did a shitty job of it." His tone was matter-of-fact. "You could have walked into a trap of angry guards with guns at any point. You were fortunate, you know."

"I did not get shitty intel…" Anya cut herself off before she revealed anymore secrets she shouldn't. "I was prepared. I had it under control."

She couldn't defend his second statement at all. Of all the things she'd been tonight – cocky, stealthy, fast, defended, *caught* – fortunate wasn't one of them.

He cocked his head again, as if he could see through her secrets to the frightened part of her. "I can see that."

"Why aren't you enjoying yourself with one of the willing dates provided by your hosts?"

"But I am."

Anya gave him a swift disbelieving look.

He looked in deadly earnest.

"We're not going to…" She waved a trembling hand in the general direction of the white, white bed he was leaning against. "Do that."

"I didn't think so." His teeth were very white when he smiled like that. It, too, was disturbing.

"But, you know what?" Drake Fallahil did the strangest thing of all.

He yawned. Loud and without shame.

"I'm tired. And this is a lovely bed. So I'll see you in about…" He made a great show of sweeping the French cuff of his immaculate suit back and check out his watch. Cartier, if she wasn't mistaken.

"Ninety minutes," the watch announced.

Anya blinked. Did Cartier make wearables?

"Wait! What? What are you doing?" She shrieked as he removed his jacket and folded it over his arm before placing it at the foot of the bed.

"What does it look like I'm doing? I'm trying to take a nap. It's almost two am."

"But…" She tried to articulate her scattered thoughts again. "What about me?"

He gave her a speaking glance. "You can rest too. We aren't going to do…" He made the same waving gesture she'd made. "That. Your virtue is safe with me."

"I don't want to *sleep* with you," she gritted out. Aware of how unworldly and girlish she sounded. Uncaring of it. No way, no *way* was she getting onto that expanse of bed with a man.

Not this man.

Not happening.

"Well, we are supposed to be enjoying the fuck out of ourselves. Aren't we?" he reminded her coolly.

Anya threw her hands up. "It's been twenty minutes, give or take. We'd be done 'enjoying' by now, by any standard."

He leaned over, really close.

She knew it was a test. It still did not stop her from shrinking back, half-reclining on the bed.

"I don't get done in twenty minutes. Ever," he spoke softly.

But his words stirred the edges of her hair. They brushed against her cheeks, flushing them with dark, hectic color. Running down the rest of her body, pooling low in her womb. They made her peek her tongue out.

His hypnotic eyes found the action, arresting there. There was a look to him, a contained wildness she couldn't look away from.

Then, he reached around her, his warmth and strength enveloping her, while the seams of his shoulders in the hand-stitched silk strained against his skin.

Giving her a rather graphic idea of how his muscles bunched and flowed.

He took the blanket kept at the foot of the bed and dumped it on her knees. "Sleep here or on the couch. Don't. It doesn't matter. We are going to stay in here till I say otherwise."

She let out a trembling breath as he receded away from her.

Anya resolutely turned away as she felt him rustle against the bed. Finally the movements stopped.

She clutched the sheet in both hands, drawing it over her chest and shoulders.

The room was icy-cold now. With a shock, she realized Drake Fallahil had actually chased the cold away with his presence.

Her insides trembled again. Violently.

She quickly peeked at Drake Fallahil stretched out on the bed. His head pillowed on his hands, eyes closed, chest moving in a deep and even rhythm that couldn't possibly be REM sleep.

It was a big bed, she reasoned. *Big enough for the two of them.*

Anya crawled up to the other side and gingerly stretched out under the sheet. Her right side warmed quickly as if he really was a human space heater.

I'll rest for a minute. For just a minute, she promised herself. Her eyes drifted closed. And she breathed a tiny sigh out.

Before, she knew it, Anya slid into deep and dreamless sleep in her enemy's bed next to a man who was more dangerous to her than them all.

SEVEN

Drake woke up by degrees. Emerging from rest to consciousness, his brain switching on bit by bit.

First, he became aware of the light. Streaming slightly from the heavily curtained windows, a pale suffusing glow indicating not-yet dawn.

He blinked, clearing the sleep from his vision. Assimilated his surroundings—a bedroom in an apartment in Tanjong Pagar that wasn't his own.

Then, his hearing tuned in and he heard a low, snuffling sound. He turned around, his neck creaking just a bit from stiffness.

Drake saw her.

The woman he'd followed, past his own better judgment and reason. The woman who'd given him no answers to all the questions he'd asked.

She was huddled under the covers, curled on her side. Her back was to him. All he could see of her was a small mass, curved into an S on the other side of the bed.

The sound came again. A sort of sigh-snuffle.

The urge to touch her overcame his boundaries and he touched her shoulder, peeking over the covers. Lightly, at first and then with gentle urging when she didn't stir.

"Hey," he rasped out. "Hey, it's okay."

Drake moved closer to her, swinging his bulk halfway across the bed to be closer to her. He felt *weird* in a way he hadn't in some time. He attributed it to getting deep, REM sleep after weeks.

She didn't stir, just made that sound, so he tried again.

"Hey, Anika."

He squeezed her shoulder again. It was soft and warm to his touch. His fingers covering the breadth of her bones and skin which quickly heated.

She moved against his palm, sinuously. Her heart beat slow and steady and deep against him. Boom. Boom. Boom. The sound echoed in the too—quiet room.

So, he did it again. Moved his fingers over her shoulder, touching the nape of her neck. His own heartbeat was slightly sluggish, as if he was dreaming too.

"Anika." He said her name again.

The covers slid down at his repeated actions. His gaze dropped down at the tiny strap sliding down her arm, moving up and down with each deep breath she took. He traced the line of the strap moving it once, twice.

Waiting for her to wake up. Acknowledge him. Or slap him for invading her privacy.

Finally, she turned her head and opened her eyes. Fragile lids quivering open, her lashes feathered against her cheeks, as if they were too heavy to rest up. Her dark eyes were unfathomable, hazy in the dim light.

"Anika," he breathed.

She said nothing.

He touched the strap again, pulling it down, down so more of her curves were revealed.

She lay still and passive, like a doll. It shouldn't have aroused him but it did. As if she *trusted* him to not hurt her, touch her in any way she couldn't handle.

As if he trusted himself too.

"Tell me if you don't want this." The words came from that part of his conscience that still lived on. Struggling against the monster every minute.

"Tell me, okay?" He touched his lips to her fragrant arm.

She moved, a lazy action, her spine bending a little.

Drake kissed up her hand to her shoulder, to the sweet hollow of her ear, pushing her hair out of the way. His own hair swinging to brush against her skin. Goosebumps raising all over his skull at the slight contact.

She made a sound. A sort of broken moan.

He kissed her again, a hot, open-mouthed kiss against the soft curve of her ear. Drowning in the very give of her.

Later on, he would think that she turned her head, bending her neck, seeking his mouth. Demanding it, even.

But the truth was, in that moment, he clutched her closer, so he was half-lying over her. Already aroused to the point of pain, his fingers digging into the fleshy part of her arm, turning her into his heat and strength.

She didn't resist him, which served as good as a yes to him in that hot, heady moment.

She just stared up at him.

A mute nymph he'd somehow caught in his arms, right when dawn met night. Her hair flowing like rivers of black ink on the white pillow, her body slight and pliant against his. Her curves fitting against his leanness as if they were two puzzle pieces of a whole.

His eyes burned, he *felt* them burn as he stared down at her.

Then she brushed his hair back from his cheek and he felt the slight brush of her fingers down to his toes. It was intoxicating.

When he bent down to kiss her, unable to help himself, she lifted hers. They collided, somewhere between dawn and night, soft against hard. He kissed her reverently, with gentleness he didn't know he possessed. As if to soothe some wildness in her that he understood.

It made no sense to him. Save that he could do it forever.

Her lips weren't just soft, they were petal-soft. Their taste wasn't just sweet, it was ice cream left to melt in the sun. It was addictive. She opened her mouth and he was lost, cupping her shoulders so they were pressed together, torso to torso.

His tongue swept in, seeking, searching…when he found hers, *he* was lost. Lost in her taste and feel. Sucking it into his own as if he could somehow enfold the taste inside him too.

Drake changed angles, so he could kiss her deeper, take more. Their tongues tangling, their lips melded together in a deep, open, endless mating. Taking whatever he could take.

No sound emerged from him, as his breath was stolen, claimed…

Her hand came up, hovering between them.

Then she pushed at his shoulder. Once, twice.

Drake lifted his head, lips parted, muted by the intensity of whatever *this* was.

"Stop," she whispered. Tears shimmered in her eyes.

He immediately stopped.

~~~~~~

Anya couldn't breathe, she couldn't move her chest enough to allow her lungs to decompress. It felt as if all her blood had stopped cold, turning to ice the second
~~~~~~

Drake Fallahil moved his warmth away. As he did what she'd asked, the second she'd asked.

Stopped.

Kissing her.

Touching her. Overwhelming her.

At first, it had been a dream. The most pleasant of dreams, having someone, *him* touch her shoulder. So gently, kindly as if he all he cared about was her comfort. It turned worse, made unspoken wants and foolish dreams bubble to the surface when he'd turned her in his arms, his length surrounding her, making her feel safe and protected and *alive* at the same time.

She'd opened her eyes and seen him.

This man who did not belong in her world at all. He belonged to that misty space where reality and dreams met each other and melded into the impossible. He wasn't *real.* Those eyes which drew her in like a beacon, homing in on her till she felt seen. As she'd never been seen before.

Anya fell into his eyes before a word was spoken between them. Before his lips on her skin drowned her.

It seemed so natural, necessary even to have him kiss her arms, so they turned weightless. And then he kissed the tender shell of her ear, his lips scraping against her skin there. And it was unbearable, too much. Her breasts peaked and she felt an ache deep in the pit of her stomach, where emptiness yawned like a great beast awakening.

He kissed her again and again while the rest of her turned weightless. Looking at her as if she mattered, so she had to…just had to push his hair back as it caressed his hard cheek.

And then, then his lips covered hers. And the want went from unbearable to untenable.

Anya was aware of every micro-sensation. The scrape of his beard against her chin. The pads of his fingers touching her shoulders, pressing her closer. The individual buttons of his shirt digging into her slip, imprinting their shape and his heat on her body.

She floated, dreaming yet or wanting to, as he kissed her perfectly. Exactly as she'd always wanted to be kissed. With gentleness and a soothing passion that ignited all the fires in her skin. As if she'd been made to kiss and touch him. Only this man.

Her brain, ever her saving grace, tripped awake at this point. And she pushed at his shoulder. Once, twice. Ruthlessly squelching all pleasure at how firm, how un-giving his sinew was under her touch.

"Stop," she whispered.

Tears spurted into her eyes at the beauty and grace she'd just experienced. And it was heartbreaking that it was with *this* man.

He stopped immediately.

She sat up, trying to contain all the feelings running riot inside her. Chief among which was deprivation.

"I did ask if you wanted this," Drake pointed out quietly.

Anya nodded, tugging her dress into place, only more brutally aware of the ways he'd touched her. The warmth of his palms and fingers sunk into her skin, to live there forevermore.

"I didn't mean to lead you on," she returned, just as quietly.

"You didn't, sweetheart." He left the bed and opened the door, poking his head out.

Abruptly, she was aware of the line of his lithe body. Strong, straight, the belt digging into a trim waist and the width of his shoulders even more apparent without the expensive jacket.

She wanted to touch those shoulders. Having him hold her close.

The want alarmed her. Shamed her.

It was that shame which made her snap out, "Well, then you shouldn't have touched me in the first place. I like to be memorable, you know."

Drake Fallahil stilled. He shut the door slowly and leaned against it, crossing his arms against those impressive shoulders. A look on his face that turned her blood cold anew.

Anya wanted to apologize. She wanted to take her words back. Because she'd never seen a man look so blank and in control at the same time.

"Is that the case?" he asked.

"Look." She stood up from the bed, dropping the sheets in a hurry. Her legs wanted to buckle from the force of his stare, halfway across the room. But she still had some pride left. "That wasn't well-done of me. I'm sorry."

"You owe me twenty-two thousand SGD worth of sorries," he offered sardonically.

She flinched because it was nothing but the cruel truth. "I told you, I can't afford to pay you back." In her agitation, she'd actually folded the sheet and placed it neatly at the foot of the bed.

When she straightened up, there he was.

Right next to her. "I didn't ask you to," he said calmly.

She carefully stepped back from him.

He leaned down to pick up his jacket from the counterpane. Wore it with economical movements.

Anya noted the two steel-gray monogrammed buttons on his cuff. "So, what do you want with me, then? I mean…there were hundreds of women at that party. You could have been with any one of them. They'd be a lot more…accommodating of you."

"And cheap. Don't forget cheap," he said coolly.

Her hands clenched at her sides. "And cheap," she agreed woodenly.

He gave her another searching gaze which she did her damndest to hold without dropping her own eyes.

"Are you going to tell me now what you were doing here tonight?"

Anya shook her head. "No."

She was so weary, her head ached. Her whole body ached. She wanted a shower, her mother's egg curry and rice and she wanted to sleep till the memory of this night was forever relegated to her dreams.

Wishful, impossible dreams…

What he said next almost broke her.

"I could help you, you know."

The very worst part was how gentle, how non-judgmental he was. Not angry or upset. What was that word he'd used – *thwarted*.

No, he was very much a man. A lovely man with a lovely heart who'd paid an ungodly sum of money to get her out of a tricky situation.

To ask him for even more help, to make him accessory to her own crime was a non-starter.

~ ~ ~ ~ ~

"Thank you," Anya said politely. "That is very kind of you. But I don't need any help."

"I see."

She peeked at him then, unable to not look.

He *was* lovely. And not because of the way his features were put together or the his extraordinary eyes or even how freaking rich he looked. Wealth had a look, a smoothness of the skin and a straightness of bearing, a confidence that came from knowing you had enough to cushion and weather whatever came your way.

No, it was because of how he made *her* feel. Just being in the same room with her.

Lovely.

"No," she said shortly. "You don't."

She took the four steps required to move past him when he caught her hand. It was a classic gesture, one of romance and arrogance.

He simply did it as fact. Circling her wrist with his fingers in a grip that wasn't tight at all. She could break away, free, any second she wanted.

But Anya turned. Like he wanted her to. And she gave him another look. This one impatient, slightly annoyed. But, all the same, she looked.

"What now?"

"Maybe you don't need my help, but what if I do?"

"What is the great Drake Fallahil in need of?"

"A wife," he answered casually.

"And you might as well do."

EIGHT

If Anika was shocked at the words that came out of his mouth, it was nothing compared to the earthquake that went off inside Drake the moment he said them.

Had he just asked this strange nymph of a woman to marry him? Had he lost his goddamn mind?

Utter, awkward silence reigned supreme in the room after his declaration.

Drake opened his mouth to…breathe, curse, *say* something but the woman beat him to it.

"That's preposterous," she said coldly. "Even for a man like you."

Now it was his turn to stare at her, bemused. Was there a man like him? "A man like…"

"You think you can buy anything, don't you? Even people?"

"What?"

"Just for a second there, just for one fucking second," she muttered furiously, "I thought you were okay. Not good. Not sweet. Just *okay.*" She arranged her hair in a tight bun that elongated the long line of her neck.

He didn't want to pay attention to it, or the way her shoulders bunched and flowed.

He couldn't stop looking at her. Now, that was preposterous.

"But clearly, men like you and Ajay Runwal…you are above the rest of us. Us ordinary, working class people. You give orders and the world obeys. Because you have money." She poked at his chest so hard he actually took a step back. "And power. And you wield it like it's your right."

She spit the last word out.

"Look," he began placidly, his head spinning.

"NO!" The word exploded from her mouth. "I am going to do my damndest to pay you back the money you used to bribe those guards on my behalf. Or die trying." She wore one of her ice-pick shoes while he took another careful step back. That thing was pointy.

"But, if you think I am going to allow you to treat me like I'm a…a…*commodity.*" She wore the other shoe. "Just because you paid off those goons, then allow me to disabuse you of that notion right fucking now."

She brushed past him on slinky heels, yanked the door open, fairly vibrating from the force of her anger.

"I wouldn't marry a man like you if you came to me on bended knee with a rose stuck between your teeth. You can't afford me, Mr. Fallahil."

Then she slammed the door shut so hard it vibrated through him.

~ ~ ~ ~ ~

After five thrumming seconds of quiet, in which Drake attempted and failed spectacularly to make sense of a world gone wrong, he took the first step towards rationale. He pressed a button on his watch and called his car up to the parking entrance of this misbegotten apartment.

Fortunately, or unfortunately, he was met with two guards as he was exiting the elevator at the underground car park.

"You're not supposed to be here, man." Guard one spoke while guard two pointed his automatic at him.

Drake didn't even pause to think, he just grabbed the barrel of the M16 rifle from the guard, and yanked it so the man was off-balance. Then he kneed him for good measure, getting him in the gonads. The guard went down in a pained grunt.

By the time the other guard thought to point his own gun at Drake, Drake had already leveled the business end of the M16 at the man's forehead.

"I squeeze," he said softly. "You die. Is getting fired from this job worth you dying?"

The man immediately raised his hands in the universal gesture for surrender. His gun slung back to his shoulder, as he checked on his groaning friend.

Drake gave him a considering glance. "You've got good self-preservation instincts. I could use a man like you on my staff. Come see me when Runwal fires you. Okay?"

The man nodded rapidly, muttering or cursing in the local language – Malay.

Drake handed the gun to the man, butt-first, and walked out, hands in pocket instantly feeling better about being himself. He was actually whistling when the car showed up at the kerb. It was a local electric SUV with a reinforced chassis and bulletproof glasses.

He even smiled pleasantly at the woman with the mile-long legs who stepped out of the vehicle. Holding a large travel mug of his favorite coffee and a larger bottle of spring water.

She tossed her pin-straight hair back as she handed both to him.

"Thank you, Mili." He kissed her cheek. "You're a life-saver. Best assistant ever."

~ ~ ~ ~ ~

"I live to serve you. Why are your knuckles scratched?"

Drake checked his hand out. Yes, the skin was marred. He gave her a wink. "I got into an altercation with the Runwals' security. The guy might come looking for a job later on. Have him assigned, will you?"

"These altercations wouldn't happen if you had a body on you, Drake," Mili muttered. "I don't understand why you won't hire security for yourself, or a damn PR firm to handle your life."

"Because." He twisted the coffee cup in his hand, flexing it. "I have one life to lead. And finally, it's mine to lead here. I'm not Chairman of Fallahil Holdings Inc anymore." Drake dismissed the last two decades of his life with three sentences. "I am starting up again. I'd like to do so on my own terms. No more managed life for me, Mili."

"That's deranged," Mili commented. "Sir."

Drake's smile widened as he chugged half the coffee down, allowing it to burn his throat. Burn away all the absurdity of the dawn. Burn every fine feeling he'd momentarily experienced until he was what he'd always been.

Himself.

"That's because I had an interesting night," he commented lightly.

He allowed her to precede him inside the car, twisting the glass top off the bottle. He drank thirstily, uncaring that water trickled down his throat and into the collar of his suit. "That's better."

"Deranged," Mili repeated. "What happened last night?" She leaned forward, eyes narrowing in consternation. "Did Aster Chan corner you here? Her assistant told Thad she was out of the country for a girl's night out in Macau but one never knows with scorned women."

The car moved smoothly, quickly through the early morning traffic.

Drake looked out the window and thought of the scorn in Anika's eyes. His lips almost twitched into a smile. "No. Aster didn't show up to Bacchanalia. And I haven't scorned her, you know."

He didn't know why he felt compelled to make the distinction. "I just…want different things than her."

"Does she know what you're actually doing while she's out trying to screw your bottom-line?"

Drake leaned back and thought of the sheer genius of the strategy he'd employed the second she'd delivered her ultimatum. "No. She doesn't. She thinks her father will eventually love her."

"You are deranged," Mili observed. "Did you accomplish business with the Runwals, at the very least?"

He shook his head. "No, I wasn't. I was…occupied with something else."

Mili frowned. "Something more pressing than protecting your various business concerns in this country?"

Drake sipped slowly at his coffee, savoring it. Allowing possibilities to race through his mind, discarding each of them swiftly. "Yes. Well, no," he conceded. "Because nothing is more important than staying here."

"Drake, we could up stakes and leave tomorrow without you losing sweat over it. Or more than a hundred mill," Mili began reasonably. "At best."

Drake shook his head. "It's not about the money. It's the principle of the thing. I told you."

"And it has nothing to do with your giant." Her gaze dipped insolently to his crotch. "Ego?" she asked sweetly.

Drake shook his head again, more amused than offended. "Of course, I'm pissed off. I'm a farm boy from Minnesota, Mils. We had nothing but pride back where I come from. But," he stressed. "That is not why I'm intent on staying here."

"Then why?" she pressed him.

"It's home," he answered simply.

~ ~ ~ ~ ~ ~

After twenty years of traveling the world, in search of the next big deal, in search of the next zero in his portfolio, of finding and saving the world with lines of code and people smart enough to wield them, of trying to pinpoint just what exactly could make a man like him worth saving…he'd come here, a few months ago after a disastrous Christmas at Lily's in Chicago…and he'd been soothed.

In his heart. If it existed.

This tiny island nation of three million people and more green country than Georgia, had hold of him in a way he'd not wholly expected. Or was comfortable with.

When Mili said nothing cutting to his rather sentimental statement, he finished the rest of his coffee before switching to the water. "Besides, you really didn't think I'd let Aster Chan, of all people, beat me, did you?"

"Well, she has, Drake," Mili spoke slowly. Like she was talking to a small toddler. "You've got less than five days to find a woman willing to marry you and stay married to you for better or worse. And no one in this city would dare cross a Chan. All the elite matchmaking platforms have blocked you, as have the dating sites," she said bluntly. "And the sex clubs too, for that matter. Even your business deals are in danger of falling apart or have you forgotten?"

"I forget nothing, Mili."

"Then what are you doing about it?" she demanded.

"You know why I always win," Drake murmured as he recalled Anika's flashing eyes. The sheer rage in them. Not when he'd proposed to her. But when he'd bribed the guards the second time to leave them alone.

When she'd thought he was going to do something unspeakable to her.

She'd been magnificent.

"Because you use bloody game theory like a fucking rule book?" Mili muttered. "Everyone loses something but everyone wins most things so they don't care about the loss."

He shook his head. "It's because I make the one move everyone else is afraid to make because I've already lost before I begin."

He gave her a calm look and her thickly-kohl'd eyes widened because she saw the monster unfurl within him.

It craved violence and hungered for power. Whose teeth bit into his skin when he'd taken those guards down without breaking a sweat. It still wanted *more.*

Anika hadn't been that far wrong about his character. She was just wrong about the why of it all.

And he knew now, *exactly* why he'd followed her last night. Why she intrigued him so. Why he'd rescued her from the security guards and almost, almost allowed her to sneak past his own walls.

Why he'd chosen her to marry him, of all people.

She was the anomaly, the one woman in this island nation of three million people who wasn't under the Chans' influence.

Because they didn't know she existed.

"And when you know you've lost, you're not afraid anymore, are you?" He murmured, almost to himself. "You can do audacious things."

"What audacious thing?" Mili asked warily.

Drake looked out the sun-tinted window of the soundless car, which ran on electricity, made by a company he owned controlling interest in, without anyone being the wiser. He'd invested in at least four different countries pursuing electric vehicles as the main mode of transport, a decade before climate change became a watchword.

Because, he really was that far-thinking. And he really was that unafraid.

Drake thought about the genius of his plan, the sheer simplicity of it amazed even him. Because his brain had figured out a simple, elegant solution to his problem without him being aware of it.

He'd thought he wanted the elusive woman, that he was interested in *her*, when all he was interested in was cementing his position and power here in Singapore.

No, she was the means to an end. A very expensive end, of course, but nevertheless just the means to an end.

"I found the woman I'm going to marry and beat Aster Chan at this ridiculous farce of a game, once and for all."

NINE

There were few things worse than being stuck in a place with no windows. Sure, finding a simple two-line bug in four million lines of code was the worst thing but sunlight was important too.

And you didn't get sunlight when you were stuck in jail.

Ishqi Kathuria watched the massive door of the visitor's section open, and two guards – Hurly and Burly with automatic rifles and pokers-up-their-butts expressions – escorted a high-class hooker in. The hooker wore a knockoff Chanel LBD and black shoes, which proved her sense of fashion was adequate, at best.

And her hair and makeup…

Ooh, this chick had worked for her pay the night before.

Ishqi bounced her knee impatiently as she looked at the clock signifying the number of minutes draining the time allotted for her sainted sister to visit her.

Where the fuck was Anya?

"You look well," Anya spoke.

Ishqi turned in amazement.

The hooker had opened her mouth and her sister's voice came out. "They're treating you well?"

Anya toed off her shoes and sat down in the chair opposite Ishqi.

"Fuck, Anya." Ishqi leaned back and whistled empty air through her teeth. "I couldn't recognize you at all. I thought you were some escort who'd come to visit her prison girlfriend." She smiled thinly. "And if I can't recognize you, your own sister, there's no fucking way the Runwals did. Am I right?"

Anya twisted the top off a bottle of spring water and rotated it between her fingers. "No," she said at last. "No one recognized me."

Ishqi leaned forward, eager to hear the rest of the good news. "That's awesome, sis. I didn't think you had it in you to pull this off but…" She waved a hand up and down at Anya's breasts so clearly defined in the dress. "You have. So spectacularly well."

Anya gulped down the water. "It was a nightmare, Isqhi," she said fervently.

Her eyes, a strange brown-black, glinted with unshed tears. Her chest heaved with suppressed emotion. Even her hair seemed to be standing on end, as if guarding against an invisible threat. "It was a fucking nightmare and I'm not repeating it again. Not even for you."

"You wouldn't have to, if you did what you were supposed to in the first place," Ishqi reminded her icily. "Right, Anya?"

Anya said nothing. Her lips firmed up even more, like they had when they were kids and Ishqi wanted an extra Tim-Tam and it was Anya's job to keep her away from the cookies.

"Right? Anya?" Ishqi prodded her again.

~ ~ ~ ~ ~

Anya looked around the room, particularly eyeing the guards patrolling the edges of the room. She leaned forward, and spoke in a furious whisper, "I was able to get in using the Bacchanalia girls as cover. And you were right about where the door was located, Frida Kahlo it was. And I used my clothes to blind the cameras."

"This is great, sis. I'm proud of you."

"But…" Anya bit her lip. "Your source didn't tell you about the motion sensor force field, did they?"

"What?"

Anya's voice turned into a sub-vocal whisper. "Runwal's computer is protected by a sensor force field that is defused only with his touch. It was a miracle I'm not in here, next to you, on breaking and entering and grand larceny charges, Ishqi."

Ishqi's eyes narrowed. She had light green eyes, courtesy of her father, unlike Anya's serviceable brown.

She'd always prided herself on being the more exotic sister, along with being the smarter one, of course.

"What are you saying, sis? That you didn't get the information we need to free me?"

Anya shook her head, her eyes wide and exasperated. "Did you even pay attention to what I just said, Isqhi? I could have been caught for trespassing. They'd lock me up with just cause. It was a fucking miracle I wasn't."

"How did you pull that off, Anya?" Ishqi bit off.

Anya looked down, displaying the first signs of discomfort. "Someone helped me very kindly. H…They got me out of a tricky situation." She bit her lip, with a frown. "I don't know how I'll ever repay them."

"That is not your problem, Anya," Isqhi snapped. "I'm *stuck* here." She pointed at her chest, covered in a light blue coverall, courtesy of Singapore National Prison. "And I can't get out till we find the evidence that proves definitely that Ajay Runwal hired me to work on his behalf. Do you want your sister to be stuck in prison for a crime she didn't commit?"

Anya flinched, sucked in a breath, shoulders slumped.

Ishqi felt a flicker of murderous rage at her. She looked so *wounded,* as if Ishqi had hurt her with her words. When it was Ishqi who was suffering every goddamn minute of every day that she was stuck her in this place with no windows and sunlight.

That was a nightmare.

"I'm trying," Anya spoke in a low voice. "Mom and I are collecting the funds required to retain that lawyer you need, Isqhi. Just give us a few more days."

"I don't have a few more days, do I? What if I get shivved in here, for refusing to trade a bar of soap for some cigarettes? How are you going to sleep then, sis?"

Anya's slumped back straightened. As if she was stitching herself back together bit by bit. "I won't let that happen. Mom won't let that happen, Ishqi. Why would you say that?"

"Because I trusted you to do this for me," Ishqi said softly. "I trusted you to protect me, Anya. And you failed."

Anya shook her head, and more of her ridiculous up do slid down. She wiped away streaming eyes, leaving her stupidly young face with a streak of mascara. Ishqi said nothing about the makeup, taking vicious pleasure from seeing her sainted sister unravel.

"I will do whatever I need to, to get you out, Isqhi. Please, trust me. I'm sorry," she whispered brokenly. "I'm sorry I failed you."

She reached one hand out and waited for Ishqi to take it.

Ishqi squeezed it, resisting the urge to scratch her sister's perfect skin. The bitch had access to moisturizing hand cream while Ishqi had to beg for a bar of fucking soap.

It was *unfair.*

"It's okay," Ishqi said. "We had faulty intel on the computer, didn't we?" she patted her hand. "And, at the very least, you didn't get caught or sent to jail. Who did help you out, Anya?"

Anya gave her a quick assessing look from under hooded lashes. "Would you believe it if I told you it was the richest man in the country?"

Ishqi grinned. "Unless it was Mark fucking Zuckerberg, I'd find that hard to believe."

"It wasn't him," Anya murmured.

"Then who? I'm curious now."

Anya shrugged. "He didn't give me his name actually. But he was someone powerful."

"I bet. Bacchanalia is not for the weak of heart or status," Ishqi remarked. "Or net worth."

Anya nodded slowly. "Yeah, that was abundantly clear within five minutes of reaching the penthouse." She gave a tentative smile that Ishqi returned with a measure of equanimity. "I think there was talk of bringing a tiger to wrestle an MMA fighter later on in the night."

"Yeah. These people are crazy and entitled."

"That they are." Anya sighed. "Mom's going to be heartbroken."

"You can tell her it's your fault," Ishqi said lightly.

Anya gave her a startled glance.

"I'm joking. God. Prison hasn't taken away my sense of humor, you know," Ishqi muttered, peeved.

Anya squeezed her hand between both of hers. "I promise you. You'll be out of here soon."

A buzzer sounded, signaling the end of their visit.

Ishqi rose up and so did Anya. In her heels, Anya was toe to toe with Ishqi, in her paper thin running shoes. They hugged awkwardly with the cuffs on her hands, and chained around her waist.

"I'll see you next week? Do you think you could arrange the money for the lawyer by then?"

Anya nodded. "Yeah. Okay. I'll do it."

"I love you, sis." This time Ishqi's smile was genuine. Heart-felt.

There weren't many things Anya was good at, because Ishqi was better at them all. But Anya was stupidly loyal and she had more integrity in her little finger than most people had in their blackened hearts.

So, when she gave her word it was as a good as a vow.

"Great." Ishqi squeezed her shoulder. "I trust you to take care of me, Anya."

Anya gave her a wan smile and asked, "Do you want to tell Mom anything?"

"Yeah, take care."

Anya nodded and then left, holding her shoes in her hands. Ishqi was escorted back to her cell where she waited to see if the coast was clear. Then, she flipped the sheets off her prison mattress. And stuck her hand in the middle of the gaping tear in it.

She came out with a burner phone.

Quickly, she typed out a text in utter gibberish. Pressed send and waited for a response from the sender.

Okay. I'll wait before moving. For now. Thanks for getting control of the website back to me, heart girl.

This was the response that came back.

Ishqi stuck the phone back and smoothed the sheets into place. She even lay down on the bed to cover it up.

You won't have long to wait, love, she thought. *My dumb sister is going to get me out of here as fast as her guilty conscience allows her to.*

It would have all been a grand joke if Ishqi wasn't stuck in prison.

~~~~~~

Anya was numb by the time she took the MRT back to the nearest train stop near her neighborhood, Little India. The conversation with her sister increased her headache to biblical proportions and she shivered endlessly from her abbreviated outfit.

She also cursed herself for forgetting those damn stockings at the Runwals' apartment. With *Drake motherfreakin' Fallahil.* At least they'd chase the infernal cold in her body anyway.
~~~~~~

Flagging down a cruising taxi she could ill-afford, Anya tucked her feet under her knees and out of the death-trap shoes. The meeting with her sister had gone as badly as she feared it would go. And she was left feeling as she always did.

Guilty. Responsible. *Helpless.*

The automated, solar-powered streetlights switched off at the first sign of true morning sunlight. Mustafa Center, the mecca of hoarders and shoppers from India, especially, was choc-a-bloc full of customers. It sold everything, from batteries to entire bowling alleys, and was a regular haunt for the thrifty middle-class.

Anya had a job in a small washer company in a tiny lane off Mustafa Center, in the customer service department. It was one of two jobs she held while also attending b-school full-time.

Although, if last night had gone even slightly more haywire, she'd have been out of both jobs and her bright future as an MBA graduate from the most prestigious school in the country, harder to get into than Harvard.

"We're here, ma'am," the kindly Sikh driver rumbled in his thick accent. He'd stopped in front of a cramped apartment building in a bylane off Little India's most famous restaurant – Kamath's.

Anya got out, swinging out her shoes in one hand, yawning behind the other. She paid the man, adding a five percent tip, all she could afford. Then she took her aching, miserable body up four flights of stairs to an apartment, with a welcome design of lotuses and triangles and swirls, a rangoli, done in acrylic colors. Since, this was Little India, the landlord and neighbors did not mind ethic decorations and knick-knacks.

In fact, one of the downstairs tenants, the Tiwaris, regularly held firework celebrations for all sorts of festivals, like the new moon and full moons in August, June and more.

Anya did not care for any of the celebrations, since she'd long ago decided institutional religion was a crock that denigrated women and non-men. And any god that demanded chastity and rigidity of thought and deed was not her god, at all.

But, she was a huge fan of all the food the Tiwaris and the Mukherjees and the Pandits cooked, for all the many festivals they celebrated.

Anya carefully stepped over the design, ensuring her feet did not touch the rangoli, as she unlocked the door to her apartment.

The entrance corridor was narrow and cramped and one wall was crammed full of the idol pictures her mom still worshipped faithfully – Laxmi, Saraswati, Hanuman, and Shiv jostled for space with Buddha and Mother Mary. Her mom was a catch-all devotee. She claimed there was always one more god to pray to.

Anya never could understand her mother's faith in the gods, especially when they'd ensured Swati Mallya-

Bhatt had the hardest life ever. She'd come to Singapore as a new bride to a banker, only to have her husband drop dead of a heart attack two years into the marriage. She was pregnant with a daughter by then, and had turned to her husband's best friend for solace and comfort in a new, strange land.

That man had taken advantage of Swati's innocence and desperation, cleaned out her husband's life insurance claim and her wedding jewelry, and left her with another daughter in her belly before hightailing it out of town.

It was enough to turn the most devout person into a non-believer, but not her mother. No, Swati carried on with her prayers and her poojas (godly rituals) as if others had it worse than her.

Anya shook her head off the bad memories and almost walked past the alcove leading into the living room.

The living room was a tiny excuse filled with a huge, sagging couch that had seen better days with upholstery done up by Swati, Anya's mom. A plasma screen flickered a Hindi soap opera while her mom slept on the couch, crouched into herself.

Anya immediately rushed into the room, ignoring the ache in her arches.

She shook her mom awake, lightly. "What are you doing here, mama? Why aren't you in your bed? This is bad for your knees. Don't you know that?" Anya fussed over her mother, while her own body protested.

Swati gasped as she tried to sit up, catching her right hip instinctively. She gave her daughter a bleary look. "What time is it, Anu?"

"It's early for you, mama. Go back to sleep. In your bed." Anya assisted Swati from the couch and, holding her waist, paced her steps to her mom's slower ones as they made their way to Swati's bedroom.

Swati yawned loudly and brushed Anya's hair back. "You look so tired, *beta*. What time did you get home?" She frowned, looking years younger in that one gesture. "Did you just get home, Anya?"

"I went to visit Ishqi. We had a good chat."

Anya fluffed up her mom's sheets as she deposited her on the embarrassingly small queen bed with the old but clean sheets. She couldn't look her mother in the eye and lie convincingly about her escapades of the night before.

"Oh. How is she? Is she eating enough? Is she okay?" Swati asked eagerly, settling herself with a pillow at the back.

Anya smiled wanly. "She's Ishqi, queen of all she surveys. I wouldn't be surprised if she had a blackmail racket going on with the guards."

Swati laughed. "Don't make fun of your sister while she's in jail, Anya."

Anya wanted to weep. Her mother was defending the criminal while the good girl, the dutiful daughter had spent the night doing unconscionable things with a man almost twice her age. A sexy, beautiful, insanely *hot* man.

"Anya? Are you okay? Why are you sighing?" Swati asked, hiding a yawn behind her hand.

Anya shook her head. "Nothing, mama. Get some sleep. I'll crash too. We can talk later. Okay?"

Swati nodded, squeezing Anya's outstretched hand. "Were you…successful, in your mission?"

Anya's lips twitched. "Mission, mama? Are we in a military movie?" She continued before her mother could retort. "It went…well. I have a plan."

"Of course, you do. My girls are the best and brightest," Swati murmured sleepily.

Anya squeezed her arm and left Swati sleeping, closing the door behind her. She was so tired, she almost didn't take a shower and wipe off the grime and makeup off herself. Almost kept the marks made by Drake Fallahil, billionaire investor who'd gone off the grid six months ago, on her shoulders, her waist.

But common sense prevailed and, after a brisk toweling, she wore a ratty nightshirt and boy shorts. Climbed into her own functional queen bed with a depressing brown coverlet, setting the alarm on her phone for six hours from now.

Her supermarket job began at eight pm and she wanted to finish the ethics paper by then, if she could.

I need a wife and you'll do...I could help you. Drake Fallahil's quietly ludicrous words echoed in her ears.

Anya turned her head away. He couldn't help her. No one could.

She was stuck with a felon sister who thought herself an arrogant genius and a hopefully naïve mother who couldn't move without wincing since she had rheumatoid arthritis in both knees. She was the normal one, the boring one...the one who had to bail them out.

That's just the way it was.

And no amount of wishing or sighing or thinking about the most unattainable man on earth, a man she'd never see again by the way, would change that.

Anya closed her eyes. And forced herself to sleep while dreaming practical dreams.

TEN

"That woman has cock-blocked your four billion deal with the Chengs. Are you really going to let her get away with it?" Mili Iyer spoke truculently.

I wouldn't if I knew her name. Drake turned a moody gaze at his assistant. She came up to his shoulders with her spiral stilettos and power suit with a slit on the thigh, but she was one of the few people he was a little afraid of.

"Mili," he began impatiently. "I don't have time…"

"Four billion," Mili reminded him idly. "It was a solar farm with wind energy components in the middle of some of the most uninhabitable land in Southern Asia. Guaranteed to provide thousands of jobs. This was the deal the woman cock-blocked."

The car dropped them off at the entrance of the Chan wing of the illustrious National University of Singapore. The school's business program was considered to be the best, bar none. Not even Harvard.

And Drake had been cordially invited by the Dean of International Finance for a mixer with some of the most promising students in this year's cohort.

Drake gave an exasperated glance. "Remind me why I hired you if you're just determined to make me feel like shit when I already feel so much like shit? Also, why am I talking to a bunch of kids when we should be problem-solving for Chan?"

Mili – with an IQ rivaling his own and a string of degrees she'd obtained while also working for him – snapped the top off a caffeinated drink and handed it to him.

"You're talking to a bunch of bright young adults on the cusp of doing something phenomenal. And because you just donated a sum equal to that of the Chans plus five to this university, to start building your street cred. They wanted you to inaugurate a bust in your honor. I talked them out of it. Because I anticipate your needs." She was demure. "Sir.

Drake took the drink she held out and drained half of it in one go. "You're not that good, Mils."

"I am." She tapped one ear to her air-buds. "Iyer for Fallahil. No, he's not available for a meeting tonight. I don't need to see his schedule to know it thoroughly. Thank you so much, Mayor."

She ended the call while Drake swirled the rest of the drink in his hand. "I don't know what to do about Aster," he admitted. "I honestly don't."

It galled him to admit it. But there you go. He been temporarily destabilized by the antics of one woman and the disappearance of another…

Although, if Mili knew about Anika, she'd bust a gut laughing at him. Mili lived to see him brought down low.

Then again, Drake sipped his energy drink. If anyone could find out the disappearing woman it would be his most efficient assistant.

She was a sorceress when it came to procurement.

Mili tapped on her earbud and spoke, "Iyer for Fallahil. Oh, hey Shiv. Just a second, I'll patch the call through to Drake."

Mili handed him his phone, the one whose number even he didn't possess.

"Shiv, hey," Drake began diffidently.

"The answer is no," Shiv Naren Pal, hacker extraordinaire said bluntly. "Whatever your ask is, my answer is 'I'm retired from the hacking business. So, no'."

"But you didn't know what I was going to ask, did you?"

"Does it have something to do with those nudie pictures of you and your heiress girlfriend floating around on the internet?"

Drake huffed out a breath. "Yes but."

"You're a celebrity, Drake," Shiv said reasonably. "Like a blond, blue-eyed Musk, or so Naina tells me. With great fame comes great visibility."

"Thank you for the morality lesson, Shiv. And how long ago was it that you told your brother Kit…that he *was* your brother, Kit?" Drake asked morosely.

Shiv chuckled. "I'm not even going to pretend to be surprised that you know that. What I am going to say is this. It's just a picture on the internet. Don't worry about it."

"I'm not," Drake reassured him dryly. "I'd just like to punish the person responsible for putting me in this infernal position."

"Do tell," Shiv was too eager. "Did someone actually manage to shake down the great Drake Fallahil?"

"Fuck off, Shiv," Drake bit out.

"Easily." Shiv disconnected the call.

Drake pocketed the phone in disgust. Gave Mili a befuddled look. "He hung up on me. The man hung up on me."

Mili shrugged. "Happens, when you tell someone to fuck off. They do."

Drake gave her a myopic glance. "Any other helpful suggestions, Mili?"

"You know, we wouldn't be in this position if you'd do as I suggested when we first got here and got a body on you."

"A bodyguard?" Drake shuddered. "We discussed this. I'm not royalty, Mili. I'm a hard-working businessman."

"Then, do as she asks," Mili suggested. "Marry someone. Pay them if you have to. And be done with it. It's the easiest and most efficient solution. And no." She shook her perfectly coiffed head before Drake could voice the thought in his head. "I'm not marrying you. Not for all the money in the world."

"Why not?" He was only idly curious.

"Because you're a brigand and a monster," she answered bluntly. "Except you're the nicest monster I prefer to have in my corner."

"I'm not a monster. I'm trying to change the world, you know," Drake protested. "Aren't I here to inspire fire and passion among the bright young minds?"

They opened the frankly pretentious doors to the room where the Dean waited for them. The room was full of people in their Sunday best and cameras started popping and flashing the second Drake and Mili walked in.

They didn't care, as they were both used to it. But Drake could never understand the urge to share every single minutae of your life online. He'd profited off it, of course, having invested in three different social networks before it became a two-hundred billion dollar industry.

But he never understood the need to snap, tweet, and insta meeting anyone important.

"You are. But you don't care enough about the world to live in it. Marrying you would be committing emotional suicide. Find someone else desperate enough to do so, Drake," Mili advised.

Coming to a decision, Drake turned to Mili. "I need you to do something for me."

"Consider it done," Mili answered promptly. "They are clapping for you. Wave at them."

Drake blinked and waved around the room. He could vaguely hear the thunderous applause that greeted him as the whole place erupted.

For him.

He knew it, had heard this sound hundreds of times, thousands even, every time he walked into a room or a stage…announcing dividends during stock meets at the VC firm or design conferences for tech companies he'd helmed from the group up.

Any other man would have enjoyed the sound. Reveled in it.

It was proof he'd had it made.

Drake only thought of the loss of thousands of jobs because Aster Chan wasn't getting her way. And he considered marrying her to shut her up.

But Mili was right. Marrying him was committing emotional suicide…

"Mr. Fallahil," Dean Ashok Sharda pumped his hand enthusiastically. "We are beyond honored that you'd grace us with your presence today."

Drake smiled, continued the handshake. "It's my pleasure, Dean Sharda. Anything for the students. They are our future, you know. If I'm as smart and astute as I'm known to be, one of these bright people possesses the next billion dollar idea," he pitched his voice higher, including the whole room in his chatter.

"And everyone knows. I like to invest in those people and their ideas, don't I?"

The applause deafened even him but he smiled and waved and played the part of benevolent benefactor… all the while knowing it for the charade it was. He wasn't benevolent, he was no one's benefactor.

He was as selfish as they came.

And he was okay with it.

~~~~~~

"I'll see you after class," Anya told her mom. "I don't have to go to work till seven."

Swati's lips trembled. "Can you…are you going to see your sister?" she asked softly.

Guilt, that complicated and omnipresent emotion, rose its gleeful head up. Pinched at Anya's heart when she saw the unfettered hope on her mom's lined face.

Swati was so nice to the criminal daughter sitting in jail.

Anya wanted to scream at her until she was blue in the face. But it would do no good. It would only make her
~~~~~~

mother cry, add to the pain in her life. And she already had enough to contend with.

So Anya bit back her harsh words and slowly shook her head. "I'll see her next week," she explained carefully. "There's been a slight…glitch in the plan."

Swati knew the bare bones of what Anya had done on Friday night but she'd deliberately kept the details vague. No need to make her mother an accessory to grand larceny and cybercrime if she could help it. Of course, her mother hadn't protested at all when Anya had told her the bare bones she had.

All she wanted was for her other daughter to come home.

Anya was expected to bring her home. It was the unspoken hope in her mom's eyes.

Now that hope dimmed a little. "Oh. I see."

"It's going to be fine," Anya reassured her. "You'll see." She gave her mother a quick and bright smile. "I have it all under control."

~~~~~

She had nothing under control, Anya reflected wearily as she finished her banana breakfast on the MRT, which trundled as quickly as it could towards her school, National University of Singapore.

The plan was a disaster.

She'd lost her only chance to get into the Runwals' home and now her sister was going to rot in prison
~~~~~

forever. If she was honest with herself, Anya wasn't sure it wasn't fitting punishment for her sister.

And she was tired. Exhausted. Down to her very bones.

After waking up yesterday, she'd spent the day trying to pound out the ethics paper and sent it with minutes to spare on the deadline. Then, she'd gone to work bagging groceries in a double shift at the Tanjong food market, a few hundred feet from the scene of her non-crime.

She'd come home close to one am, grabbed a hasty dinner of cold rice and dal and crashed into bed.

And she was still tired.

She thought of the blessed sleep she'd had next to Drake Fallahil. How deeply peaceful she'd felt for that one second she'd opened her eyes and found his shadowed bulk next to her, on the other side of the bed.

Chaste and safe in a way she couldn't explain to herself even now.

She wanted that feeling back. It was so comforting.

But this was her real life. Working two jobs and attending classes and trying to spring her jailbird sister out before she was shivved inside the joint.

The train stopped at Lower Kent Ridge and Anya got out with the rest of the uni-going crowd.

The campus was huge, imposing. Built along Old Chinese Empire lines, interspersed with more modern structures which still felt very much a part of the aesthetic. The quad greens were full of students from at least fifteen different countries, enjoying the sunshine, playing a quick game of hackey-sack. Or sitting in clusters with their machines open, discovering the latest algorithm that could take the world by storm.

They were all with each other, enjoying the collegiate experience. Relaxed and somehow confident things would work out for them. They had bonds, invisible and undefined, which would get them through these years. Filled with weekend keggers, epic romances, and a life that was entirely un-messy.

They weren't on scholarship and on thin ice with the dean for nearly turning in three papers late, her brain mocked her mercilessly.

"Idiot," she muttered, deliberately turning away from the groups hanging out in the quad.

She ran into the Chan Building, where the International Finance department had their classes.

Today, a huge crowd was gathered at the entrance itself. She tried to push through a throng of students elbowing them out of the way.

Finally, she made it into the lecture room. It was full of the excited chatter of students and the click-click of hundreds of phone cameras going off at the same time.

Clearly, someone important had come for the mixer. She hoped it was the Chairperson of the International Bank. She had a few questions for the woman.

"He's way too hot to be a billionaire, right?" One of the girls in front of her muttered.

Anya frowned. "Who's way too hot?"

The girl waved her hand, in the direction of the so-called billionaire.

The spit dried in Anya's mouth as she followed the girl's hand to their eventual destination.

~~~~~

She'd know the lines of those shoulders anywhere. Those intense, unnerving eyes followed her in her sleep. She dreamed of his perfectly planed face. Of touching the waves of his expertly styled hair. Just his hair.

Shock and horror held Anya immobile as she saw Drake Fallahil chatting next to the Dean of her school, smiling widely. It became worse when the Dean spotted her, and waved at her.

Drake Fallahil, damn the man, followed Dean Sharda's wave. His smile polite but his eyes cool and disinterested.

Then they alighted on her, like headlights on a frozen rabbit.

Anya's heart stopped. Then started with an uneven jerk. As if she was being pulled back from death to life. She clutched her books closely to her chest.

The Dean waved at her to come forward and someone pushed her toward the two of them.
~~~~~

Anya went forward on leaden legs, a roaring in her ears so it felt like she was walking through water.

Finally, *finally* she reached the two of them.

Drake was inscrutable. His eyes completely expressionless as he gazed down at her from his superior height.

"And this is one of those bright young minds, Mr. Fallahil," Dean Sharda said. "Anya Mallya-Bhatt wrote the position paper eviscerating private HNIs' role in the 2008 subprime global crisis for our Ethics of International Finance class."

"I see. That must be some paper, then," he murmured.

Anya's head swam. Because all she could see was his eyes, those miles of blue eyes set in that distractingly handsome face. And he had charisma.

She'd known that the other night when he'd charmed the security guards before bribing them. And it was apparent, right now when he held this unruly crowd in the palm of his well-shaped hands.

Hands that had touched her as if she was vital to him...

Anya shook her head.

"Anya?" The Dean frowned in consternation.

"Are you alright?"

"Yes, Anya?" Drake enquired gravely. "Are you alright?"

Anya stumbled back, as if lightning had struck her. Hearing her name on his lips was…unsettling. "N..no…"

She couldn't talk to him. She couldn't.

"I'm so sorry," Anya gasped. She clutched at her stomach. "I'm so sorry," she repeated. "I have to." She pushed against people, this time trying to blend in the crowd "Go."

Anya ran, while the Dean who held her future in her hands called her name desperately and the smug, insufferable man who'd wrecked the course of her life stood silently.

Watching.

~~~~~

Anya made straight to the ladies' room right off the conference hall, found an empty stall. Her head swam and her stomach roiled uneasily so she bent down and voided the entire contents of her insides in the toilet.

Tears streamed down her face – both from humiliation and actual pain.

She emerged from the stall on shaky legs, unable to even hold her backpack. She slung it over both shoulders, before washing her face and mouth. She wiped her flushed and sweaty neck with scented tissues and splashed more water over her wrists.

Anya closed her eyes at the enormity of her predicament.
~~~~~

She was so fucked.

Not only had she disrespected the Dean of her school, she'd blatantly disregarded one of the most powerful men in the city. It was unheard of, what she'd done. And she'd never be able to live it down.

She could lose her scholarship!

Anya sucked in a desperate breath, straightened her back and faced herself in the mirror.

A frightened young woman with too-big eyes on a blanched face stared back. Her sweatshirt had runs at the seams and was wet under the collar.

In her street urchin outfit, she looked as far from the sophisticated sexpot of the night she'd met Drake Fallahil as Keynesian Theory was from Smith's Economics.

Idiot, she hissed at herself. *You could have brazened it out. You shouldn't have run.*

What's done was done. All that remained now was to face the music.

Eventually.

An arm touched her elbow. She turned around to see who it was.

It was A Gorgeous Woman. Her outfit screamed Rihanna channeling Oprah while her doe-color eyes were strangely compassionate.

~ ~ ~ ~ ~

"Yes?" Anya asked warily.

"Miss Mallya-Bhatt, I'm Mili Iyer," the woman began coolly. "Drake Fallahil's Executive Aide."

"I see."

The woman wore a silver chain winking with a tiny diamond on her swan-like neck and wondered if her boss had given her the gift. The woman's neck and Anya's head were at the same height.

Mili Iyer smiled, exposing orthondontically perfect teeth over caramel-colored skin. "I came to check and see if you're okay. You left the room in rather a hurry."

"I…yes. I'm fine. Thank you for your concern." Anya tried to keep her face and tone neutral. "I had a bad banana for breakfast."

"Indeed." Mili looked at Anya's wet collar.

Anya felt hot under the collar. She'd worn her comfort sweatshirt with the school logo, faded after many washings and a pair of matchstick jeans with holes in the knees. The first outfit in her clean clothes hamper.

She tried to tug the hood of the sweatshirt so it wouldn't be so apparent. "Is there something you need, Ms. Iyer?"

Mili smiled distantly. "Yes, actually. My employer would like to have a word with you. He's quite concerned about your," she gave Anya's outfit yet another glance.

Anya resisted the urge to curl her toes in her sneakers. "Well-being."

Alarm shot through Anya. "I don't think so…I mean." She backed up a step, then another, walking backward with each word. "He's a very busy man. He doesn't need to be concerned with my well-being and…"

She bumped into someone. They caught her slender shoulders in a solid grip.

"As you can see," she continued talking to Mili, whose Chanel-lacquered lips twitched in secret amusement.

"I'm totally fine," she finished.

"I can see that," Drake Fallahil commented as he spun her around and titled her chin so she had no choice but to look up at him.

"Anika," he said distinctly.

ELEVEN

Drake struggled as Anika/Anya's eyes widened in delectable distress. This close he could see the clumps of her eyebrows where she'd not bothered with mascara. In fact, he was so close he could actually see the whites of her roots showing at the very crown of her tiny head.

He was standing too close to this woman but damned if he was going to move first.

Anya looked around quickly, to check and see if anyone else had heard him call her Anika.

Mili was studying the ceiling as if she couldn't care less what her boss was doing in broad daylight!

"You're in the ladies'," Anya squeaked. "You can't be here!"

"You okay?" he asked quietly.

"I'm fine." She shrugged out of his hold.

He left his hands hanging loose at his sides, when he actually wanted to clench his fists.

Some of the fire was back in her when she continued with a brittle smile, "Thank you so much for your concern, Mr. Fallahil. But you really needn't bother with me."

"Oh, but I disagree." He grabbed her arm when he saw her shooting her expressive gaze toward the door. "We have much to discuss."

"We really don't," she gritted out.

"I'd just do as he asks," Mili Iyer advised mildly. She was tapping something on her phone without looking up. "He usually gets his way."

"That's despotic," Anya hissed out.

"He is a despot," Mili agreed.

She gave Drake a look. "You have twenty minutes before I come get you. Also, go somewhere private? We don't want a repeat of the Marina Bay pool incident, do we?"

"No," Drake agreed. "We don't." He gave Anya Mallya-Bhatt a searching glance. "Are you going to make a fuss or can I expect you to come quietly with me?"

"Are you *kidnapping* me?" She huffed out.

Mili chuckled.

Drake reined in a curse. "I'm not kidnapping you. I'd like to talk to you. In private. Although on second thoughts…"

He looked around the preciously appointed-bathroom. At the gilt-framed mirrors and the marble countertops and the silver-plated fittings. At the lush incense gently wafting other unpleasant smells out of the vents.

"This will do too."

The door opened from the outside and Anya's eyes widened in distress.

"We can't be found here. You're in the ladies' room!"

"The limo's outside," Mili offered succinctly.

"Limo it is," Drake decided.

He felt a little like a mafia thug as he placed Anya Mallya-Bhatt, whip-smart B-school student, between him and Mili as they quickly exited the wing and directly stepped into his waiting car.

Mili slid out of the car out the other side and shut the door on Anya's face.

Anya tried to dive out by grasping the handle but the car started so smoothly she didn't even know it, till Mili receded from view.

Drake waited for her to expend her energy on escape before asking her, "So, shall we talk?"

~~~~~~~

Anya clutched her backpack closer and glared at her. She started straight ahead. "What do you possibly have to talk to me about, Mr. Fallahil?"

"Does your university know that you moonlight as a high-priced escort at depraved parties?" he asked her casually.
~~~~~~~

He'd not spoken very loudly but the words rebounded in the cramped car.

Anya sucked in a taut breath. She felt thin, far more insubstantial in this swaddling outfit than she'd had wearing next to nothing. Maybe it was the messy ponytail or the no-make up dewy look or her rounded shoulder poking out of the sweatshirt.

She looked collegian.

"How old are you?" he asked bluntly.

He was afraid she was actually just some teenage wunderkind. She definitely looked that young. And he might cross a lot of lines in order to conquer the world but he'd yet to cradle snatch.

Anya/Anika's glare went nuclear. Her eyes were a molten brown that looked shot through with gold in the cozy confines of the car. "I'm not answering that, you perv."

"Never mind." Drake shook his head. "I have no way of verifying if you're lying anyway."

She gave him a death-ray glare. "You're the most influential person I know, Mr. Fallahil. There's not much you can't do, I imagine."

"Wrong," he countered. "I didn't think for a second that you were lying about who you were when we first met."

Her lush, unpainted mouth tightened. For a second he thought they were going to tremble, but they didn't.

They remained tight, closed. As if she was forcing herself to keep her mouth shut.

He gave her points for control. The only points he appreciated.

"I'm sorry, Mr. Fallahil," Anya said stiffly. "For whatever happened the other night."

He grinned. "Is this a blanket apology coming from a student of ethics?"

She grabbed the ends of her backpack and he noted, irrelevantly, that she wore no ring. In fact, she had no jewelry of any kind. No earrings, no chains not even a watch around her wrist.

"I was just…."

"Trying to steal from the Runwals using a fake identity and hoping to not get caught?"

If looks could kill…

"Are you going to tell me what exactly were you doing that night, Anya?" Her name tasted exotic and foreign… sexy on his tongue. He wanted to say it again.

That surprised him too.

"No." She shook her head. "I can't tell you." She peeked up at him, a half-defiant, half-afraid sprite dressed in street urchin clothes. "Are you going to report me to the dean?"

He couldn't understand his own reactions anymore. He actually had a call in twenty minutes, one Mili had so helpfully reminded him of. Yet here he was, enclosed in a moving car with a woman who barely looked legal and he…didn't want to go.

"Anya," he said, just for the pleasure of saying her name.

If he didn't know better he'd have thought she sucked in a breath when he did it.

"Are you in some kind of trouble? Student loans overburdening you or something?"

He wouldn't rat her out. And he couldn't blame her for taking up a lucrative side gig if that is indeed what it was. College education in a first-world country was no joke.

"No, I'm on scholarship," she replied with quiet dignity. "One I can't afford to lose, Mr. Fallahil. So, I ask again, are you going to report me to the dean?"

"No." He expelled a breath.

Her avid eyes followed the action through his chest. She hid it well enough by pretending to check his watch out. "Don't you have a meeting to attend?"

"They can wait. You're more interesting. Always."

She looked away as if she couldn't believe his words.

And, truth be told, neither could he. But there they were.

"You know, I find it hard to believe you've given me a moment's thought since…we met."

"Oh, but I have," he assured her earnestly. "I have many fond memories of that night." Like touching her silken skin, burying his nose in her hair, brushing against her breast. Kissing her on that damn bed in the Runwals' sex bedroom.

"Don't you?"

She gave him a cool look, which did nothing to dim his interest. "My fondest memory of that night is leaving." Her lashes quirked up. "You."

"Ouch." He fisted his hand over his heart. "That hurt, Anya."

Her hands clenched. As if she couldn't help herself. "Stop saying my name," she said tightly.

"Why?" He leaned close, deliberately putting her at a physical disadvantage so she was forced to tilt her head back to look him in the eye. It wasn't arousing in the least, he assured himself.

Not in the least.

Their toes touched each other, Missoni wingtips to tattered sneaker. He imagined he could hear the thumping beat of her heart over that ridiculous sweatshirt.

"Because it's not yours to say," she snapped out. "And I'd like to get out now. Please."

"Would you now?" He grinned.

This was why he hadn't raised the hammer of god to this chick. Because she was *fun*. Because she actually stood up to him in her own magnificent way. And it was…interesting.

"I would. I realize that you don't have to play by the normal rules of the world. But I do."

"I don't," he agreed. "I never play by the rules."

"What is the point of this asinine conversation, Mr. Fallahil?" She bit out, her eyes wide with adrenalin.

"The point is…I need a drink," Drake declared.

He leaned over her, and watched… as she visibly shrank back against the faux leather seats. Her back squeaking against the fabric.

Drake opened the latch on the side compartment, revealing a mini bar filled with an assortment of drinks – alcoholic and non-alcoholic. He extracted the amber decanter along with a crystal glass and tilted the bottle in her direction. "Would you like…?"

Anya violently shook her head. "No, thank you. It's ten am in the fucking morning."

"I've been awake since four, sweetheart," he said absently as he poured himself a Macallan 18. He raised his glass in a toast, "To secrets and lies."

Anya's lips tightened and she nodded at his casual button down shirt. "Why are you dressed like a normie?"

He choked on the sip he'd taken. "Why am I dressed like a who?"

"Normie. A normal person," she informed him airily. "You know." She pointed at her own jeans and then at his. "Why are you wearing regular people clothes?"

"What did you think I'd wear?"

Anya shrugged delicately. "I didn't think a man like you would even own a pair of jeans much less wear them. Or, you know, boots with tie up laces." She nodded at his workman boots.

"A man like…" Drake took a deep breath. "If I didn't know better I'd think you were deliberately trying to offend me."

"Is it working?" she shot back immediately.

He grinned, allowed the monster to prowl in his eyes. "It is. That should scare you, Ms. Mallya-Bhatt."

"I'm not afraid of you." Her voice was very small, her posture ramrod-straight when she said it.

"Oh yeah?" He tossed the rest of the whiskey back and pointed at her clenched fingers digging into the backpack. "Your fingers say otherwise, Anya."

She pursed her lips. "Stop…"

"Saying your name, I get it." Drake surveyed the empty crystal glass. "I've never understood why Waterford crystal is so expensive when it serves the same purpose as the dollar-store version." He gave her a curious look. "Have you?"

Anya nodded at his watch. "Isn't it time for your meeting? Surely it's twenty minutes already?"

He grinned. Slow. Sure. Predatory.

Drake had the incredible pleasure of watching all the bravery drain out of her.

"There's no meeting is there?" she asked dully.

"I'm Drake Fallahil, sweetheart. Even if there were, meetings don't start without me."

She closed her eyes. When she opened them, she gave him a look. Her eyes were brown, a different dark color than what they'd been the night they'd met. But they didn't have this ring of gold in them they did today.

They didn't shimmer with unshed tears as they did today.

He wasn't sucker punched by them as he was today.

Drake was moved by a strange foreign need. Both to see her cry and to wipe the tears away. "Anya…"

"What do you *want,* Mr. Fallahil?" she whispered desperately.

"I told you," he said quietly. "I am in need of a wife. Will you be mine?"

She heaved a wild breath. "Why do you insist on this absurdity?"

"It's not that absurd, you know. Everyone gets married."

"Yes," she practically yelled the word out. "To supermodels from Victoria's Secret shows or humanitarian lawyers on the fast track to a Nobel prize or…or…former pop stars. That's who people get married to."

"You just mentioned Heidi Klum, Amaal Clooney, and Victoria Beckham. All of whom are taken, I'm afraid," he pointed out gently.

Anya threw her hands up. "Exactly, my point. Those are the kinds of women men like you marry."

Drake's eyes hooded. "Those men married those kinds of women for love."

"Yes, I…" She trailed off. Stared at him as if he was an alien with two antennae. "I didn't assume you were talking about love anyway, Mr. Fallahil."

Drake toasted her with his empty glass. "And this is why your Dean is so impressed with you, her star pupil. You're freakishly smart."

She put a trembling hand to her forehead, as if she could scrape the skin off. "I feel like Alice going down the rabbit hole."

"Well, it's a seventy-second floor penthouse up in Garden Bay, if you agree to the deal. But I see your point," he finished lightly.

"I don't," she retorted fervently. "I don't see your point at all, Mr. Fallahil. And this is just the most farcical conversation ever. I realize it's funny to you, a joke…but where I come from people don't marry total strangers. And they don't marry for anything less than love. Marriage is a sacred bond, a promise between two people who risk everything to be together."

~ ~ ~ ~ ~ ~

Drake's heart felt ice-cold. She spoke matter-of-factly, but with an underlying melancholy, a bittersweet regret. As if she knew something he didn't know - wanting to take this kind of risk was insanity, but wanting it anyway.

"And all this happens in your ordinary world? Is that what you're saying?"

She heaved a heavy sigh. "No," she answered softly. "It happens in an ideal world."

"But we don't live in an ideal world, do we? We live in the real world. And in the real world…"

"You need me to be your wife," she finished for him. "You could send out a social media blast and there will be a line of prospective, interested women. Why me?"

Drake shrugged. "Why not you? You're here. You're available."

"I could have a boyfriend," she pointed out nastily.

He shrugged, allowed his insolent shrug to speak for him. He didn't give a shit whether she'd found the great love of her life. She suited his immediate purposes and he'd somehow found her without looking.

The deal was done as far as he was concerned.

"I see," she said quietly, when the silence stretched to breaking point.

"And well…not to put too fine a point on it, I caught you, Anya. I'm keeping you," he finished simply.

"I'm not a prize trout. You can't keep me," she protested.

"No," he agreed. "Prize trout you're not."

"Give me one good reason I should even consider your asinine proposal," she said coolly.

He had to give her style points. She had a mouth on her, wasn't half-bad to look at. And he could tell her the truth, the actual truth. She owed him money and his silence for not reporting her to the dean.

He didn't even have to bring up the ridiculous bet, or Aster bloody Chan and her schemes.

The truth shone in her defiant posture. In the curve of her shoulders and the way she held her neck, balanced as if a knife's edge. The knowledge was ripe in her eyes, as if she waited for confirmation that he was a ruthless brute.

He would use the knowledge of her secrets against her.

And he would.

Wouldn't he?

"Think of it as an incredible work opportunity," he said slowly.

At her startled, disbelieving glance he continued smoothly, the words smooth, practiced. Certain. "I have…a…female problem that I need to take care of. But I can't afford to offend other…parties involved with her and me. So, I need cover," he said carefully. "Having a wife would do it."

Anya hooted, the impertinent witch. "You're being stalked by an ex and you need a beard to hide from her?"

"And it *would* be an incredible work opportunity for you," he continued as if she'd not spoken. "You'd work closely with me. See firsthand how I run my interests, corporate and fund structuring are my specialties so they align with your degree too. And when we're done, I'll personally write you a letter of recommendation for any job of your choosing anywhere in the world."

"And if I said no to your incredible work opportunity? What then?" She was appropriately wary. Bitter even.

He poured himself a second glass of the amber liquid. But he didn't drink it. Just studied it, comparing it to her tawny eyes. This strange woman with her misgivings and her prickly secrets…no wonder he found her so interesting.

No one had said no to him in a long, *long* time.

"Then, I'd be forced to remind you that I could make life…uncomfortable for you, Anya." He drank the whiskey. "Are you scared now?"

"Oh, yes." She was wooden. "Petrified."

"So, the real question to answer is this, isn't it? What do you want the most in the world, Anya? Is it love? Or is it freedom? Because you'd also get a generous settlement when we dissolve our arrangement…"

"You mean, divorce. When we divorce," she inserted.

"Divorce," he said agreeably. "You'd be a wealthy young woman with the world at her feet. All you have to do is say yes. One tiny yes could change your life, Anya. Are you going to say it?"

Anya looked out the window.

Drake sipped his whiskey slowly. He knew her answer.

He could see the wheels turning in her smart head.

The same wheels turned in the head of any intrepid, fire-born entrepreneur who refused his generous funding when they were starting out.

Sometimes, he let them go. Get seeded elsewhere.

Then he'd come for the Series A, offer a stupid amount of money that would give them a two-three year runway and watch them mentally calculate how long they'd spend his money before he realized they weren't working for him.

But the truth was, when the money hit their credit line, when they started expanding…when their dreams came true because of him, they did what he wanted.

He *owned* them. Simply by giving them what they wanted.

And having the power to take it away.

But, they didn't know this. Not when they said that very first 'yes.'

"I'll never forgive you for taking my choice away," she said instead.

"I don't care as long as you choose me." He cocked his head, smiled emptily.

Anya gave him a long look. She took in his long, wavy hair, the open top button of his shirt collar, the laugh lines on his face and lips that smiled a little too readily.

And she said, what they all did. In the end. She said the only thing he wanted to hear.

Even though the odds of her saying it had been less than miniscule.

Because Anya Mallya-Bhatt had integrity pouring out of her, like perfume, or her very breath. No matter the secrets and lies she hid inside her. No matter the compromising situation he'd actually found her in.

Anya turned her head and gave him a damning look. It wasn't bitter or angry. It was…truly damning. As if he'd condemned her to hell.

She opened her defiant mouth and said, "Yes.

TWELVE

"Aster Chan is here to meet you, sir," Kimiko, Mili's aide said. "She insists on meeting you. She won't leave." Kimiko was flustered.

Drake felt a little sorry for her. Mili was a very particular boss, even worse than him sometimes when it came to dealing with the underlings. She truly was his dragon gatekeeper, when he needed her to be. Unfortunately, even dragon gatekeepers needed days off.

And Kimiko was going to catch hell for this lapse when Mili heard of it.

"Sir," Kimiko said again. "What do I do--"

"Send her in, Kimi. It's okay," he said gently.

"Mili ma'am has given me specific instructions not to." She gave him a pleading look.

"I'll tell Mili it was my idea, okay?" he added softly. "You have nothing to worry about. Just send her in."

Kimi shut the massive double doors made entirely of Italian frosted glass. They shut with a swish.

Drake considered pretending to bury his head in the file in front of him or his phone, three of which were buzzing silently, since Mili wasn't here to field his calls for him. But it was a pointless power move and he didn't have it in him to indulge Aster right now.

He was…tired, Drake realized with a start. When had he become so old as to become tired after working three days straight?

He pushed a hand through his hair, disturbing the waves. He stood up, just as the doors opened and Aster strolled in.

~ ~ ~ ~ ~

"Hello, Drake," she purred.

Drake walked around the simple glass desk he used here, to her side.

She untied her Burberry trench and he had to suck in his breath at the simple white sheath she wore under it. It was virginal in style and cut, closed high on the neck with simple puffy sleeves. It skimmed lightly over her firm and toned body and showcased her truly spectacular legs to perfection.

"Like what you see, don't you?" She handed him the coat and he hung it on the cleverly concealed plant-holder and hat stand near the doors.

Aster patted his cheek before leaning up slightly to kiss his unshaven cheek. "So do I."

She strolled further in, taking in the breathtaking view from the thirty-third floor of Oceania Park, stopping just behind his desk. The most premier of working locations in all of Singapore. It was fourteen blocks of green architecture entwined with a towering skyscraper, blending with the city's skyline while somehow standing apart from it.

"Nice view," she commented.

His office suite had three concrete walls and one glass – with the view behind his back. It showed the Quay, the Marina Bay Sands, and the tiny Lotus Temple. Singapore's pride and joy.

Aster looked down and murmured, "I can even see the Singapura Lion from here. It is a nice view."

Drake admired the curve of her back, the straight undulating line of her spine and murmured back, "It is."

She turned around, hands crossed under her breasts so they jutted into prominence. "Thank you, Fallahil."

Aster was not a falsely modest woman, she worked hard to look the way she did and spent hours on grooming and maintenance. Complimenting her was just giving her just due.

"What do you want, Aster?"

"You have forty-eight hours before your time expires. I just came to know if you've come to your senses and agreed to the inevitable."

"Nothing is inevitable, Aster." He slid his hands into the pockets of his pants, feeling the shirt stretch over his shoulders. "Except maybe me." He gave her a cocky smile that was designed to provoke her.

But Aster was a smart woman. She wouldn't fall for the obvious bait. "Why would you rent the most expensive commercial real estate here if you knew you had to leave next week?"

Drake shrugged and watched with detached interest as her febrile eyes noted the movement of his shoulders. "Maybe I'm bored and I have money to burn."

"It's because you have money to burn that you'd never do anything so frivolous, Drake. I know you," she reminded him. "No one loves to keep what's theirs than those who have everything."

"I don't have everything," he replied instantly.

The memory of a monster's belt lash stung his back. Causing him to instantly tense his shoulders and back. No, he didn't have everything if he could still regress to the helpless child he'd been once upon a long misbegotten time...

She laughed wildly. Put her arms around his stressed neck, fingered the curls on his nape.

He was stirred. Of course, he was. He was human and she was curved and toned to perfection.

"Just say the word, and you could have me, Fallahil. I'm worth it, aren't I?" She kissed his cheek again. Lingering with her perfectly shaped lips over there. "After all, I did the one thing you never expected me to."

She spoke directly in his ears. A hot, provocative whisper. "I beat you."

Drake stepped back from her, shrugging her hold off. "You have been a most worthy adversary. Fucking over my deal with the Chengs was a classic touch. Very unexpected," he commented.

Aster beamed, an angelic little smile. "I know. And it worked so much better than I thought it would. Because my father was impressed with how I undercut you, he's thinking of offering me a VP position in the company."

"Congratulations. You earned it."

"You're damn right, I did," she snapped. "Now I want my prize."

She tried to step closer to him but he danced lightly out of reach. Captured her wrists in one hand and she gave him an arch smile. "I can be your prize too."

"Aster, darling. You're forgetting something crucial. For this to be any kind of contest, I had to sign your agreement. And I didn't," he said softly. "Because this was a ludicrous waste of my time."

"We shook hands. We had a gentleman's agreement." She tossed her hair back and reminded him belligerently.

"Good thing you're not one then." He inclined his head and kissed her clenched fists. Gave her a cool look. "And I'm certainly not."

Aster's jaw dropped in disbelief. Consternation. "What are you saying, Drake? Be explicit."

"Explicitly, there's no deal. There never was," he answered quietly. "I allowed you to get away with sheer audacity, put my entire business operation in jeopardy because I get it. I get what it means to fall short. Again and again. In front of the person who's supposed to love you regardless of everything."

"I…"

"But if you, for a second, think that you beat me in this game or anything else, you don't know me at all." He leaned down and spoke in her ear now, squeezing her wrists with the slightest of pressures. Heard the harsh suck of her breath.

"While you've been playing your little game, running around town trying to block my business deals I've been in negotiations with your uncle and father. And, as of this morning, I've convinced them to give me thirty-three percent of the company." He paused for emphasis. "Your company."

Aster tried to tug her hand away while glowering at him. "You couldn't…"

"In fact, it was I who suggested hiring you in a more permanent position at Chan Holdings. Because you have a nose for ruthless business I appreciate. And I invest in the best and brightest. Always."

He gave her a thin smile which did not touch his eyes at all. Not even a little bit. Only the ruthless remained.

Drake watched patiently, quietly, as Aster connected all the dots. Saw how neatly she'd been played by him.

How she had, indeed, lost. He set her hands free, his own hung loosely.

He knew he deserved the slap she'd give him. What he had done was so breathtakingly underhanded, it deserved its own special circle of hell.

"I hate you," she spat. "You're detestable."

"I know," he agreed cheerfully. "Isn't it such a relief you don't have to marry such a detestable creature?"

Then she did slap him. Incredibly, her sloe-black eyes filled with tears she didn't allow to spill over. "I don't know how or when, Drake, but one day… I'll make you pay for this. I will."

He tugged open the doors to his office. An implicit gesture to make her exit. "You can try. Everyone tries."

She turned to say something to him, something cutting and truthful no doubt. Something he'd heard before. Because he'd heard it all. And it made no difference to him.

Drake gently shut the door on her face. Discarded her from his brilliant mind and considered the deal closed.

On an impulse, he texted Anya and asked her to meet him for dinner to discuss the specifics of their arrangement. It filled him with anticipation he didn't entirely understand as he thought of matching wits with the pixie again.

~~~~~
~~~~~

Anya was certain she'd lost her goddamn mind.

There was no other explanation for it. None.

There was no other explanation for what had happened yesterday. Because, even now, twenty-four hours later, she had a migraine the size of the 'Pura Lion roaring in her head while spots danced in front of her.

Because, even now, she wasn't sure she'd done the unthinkable. Agreed to *marry* Drake Fallahil.

The idea was preposterous. That he'd asked her. That he'd asked her twice. That she had actually *agreed!*

She'd played their truly bizarre conversation over and over in her head.

As she bagged groceries at the shopping market. Attended customer service calls for electrical appliances in a little operation right off Mustafa Shopping Center in Little India.

None of it made sense the more she thought about it, pausing over completely irrelevant details such as the way he'd held the Waterford glass so carelessly but with such apparent grace. Or his striking eyes when he'd talked about needing cover from a woman, of all things.

She'd been tempted to feel sorry for him then, because it wasn't an enviable position for anyone to be in, even bastard billionaires.

But, then, he'd tempted her with a deal that seemed too good to be true. A work opportunity with investor par none Drake Fallahil was nothing to sneeze at. He was one of the most astonishing success stories of the twenty first century, one everyone wanted to see fail.

If even half of what they'd written on his profiles were true, then he'd actually begun his investing career with winning a stake at a poker competition on Mesquita Beach one day, nineteen years ago.

She didn't believe it, of course, because it seemed… oh god, she kept coming back to that word again, preposterous.

In fact, she didn't believe anything at all.

Especially, since after she'd said yes to his proposition, he'd dropped her off at the nearest tram stop, claiming a prior meeting. He'd taken her contact info and promised, very politely, to get in touch over the next twenty-four hours to finalize details.

She'd ridden home in a total daze and refused to talk about the disastrous day she had with her mom. She'd been unable to do anything but think about the disastrous day till he'd actually texted her with instructions to come over for dinner at Oceania Park.

Of course, he'd be in Oceania Park.

She'd given an interview at one of the prestigious accounting firms in the complex last summer. It'd looked like sheer heaven. All green architecture and beautiful forms and open spaces. She didn't get the internship because she had no experience whatsoever and they wanted someone with pedigree.

She could bet they didn't have a problem with Drake's pedigree.

He'd not even bothered to *ask* her to dinner. Just plain ordered her to show up.

And she'd have to go because well…what else was she going to do? Wait for him to show up at her place of work and make her life more uncomfortable?

Anya chastised herself for thinking such unkind thoughts about a man who'd helped her out when she needed it. Badly.

And that's when she was seized with genius for inspiration.

This whole thing had begun because he'd had to pay off security guards to not snitch on her. So all she needed to do was pay him back the money he'd spent on her behalf and all would be fine.

They could forget about his insane proposition and go their separate, unlinked ways.

It was the best solution.

And so what, if her mom had kept that money for a rainy day? They were in the middle of a freaking hurricane here.

So, Anya chucked her conscience into the trash can, withdrew her mom's savings from their joint account – all twelve thousand eight hundred and twelve dollars – and set off for her one and only dinner date with Drake Fallahil.

THIRTEEN

Anya arrived on the dot of seven thirty for her appointment with Drake. She was so glad she'd worn a functional grey blazer over jeans and a pressed tee shirt with ankle length booties. And, because she was not completely without vanity, she'd slicked on gloss over her lips and lined her eyes with kohl to punch up the brown.

As she checked her reflection in the express elevator's mirrored paneling, she was confident of her business casual attire.

The doors opened and there he was.

Talking to three people, on the other side of the room.

He wore navy flat-front pants held up by a slim leather belt, hand-tooled no doubt, over a shirt the precise color of his eyes. No jacket. His hair gleamed like burnished oak in the waning sunlight. Everything about him was controlled, steady.

Yet, even from the vast distance of the room, Anya felt his power reach out and slam into her. Holding her immobile with…something.

The spit dried up in her mouth as a very real fear took root in her. One she had no name for.

He looked up from his pontificating and cocked his head to one side. "Coming?"

She held onto the strap of her backpack for strength and nodded. "Yeah."

The three people dispersed like so much wind and the room was empty but for him and her.

~ ~ ~ ~ ~

As Anya walked across the vast space she had an impression of open-ended cubicles, corner offices, walls crawling with plants and light, light everywhere. But it was just an impression.

All of her focus was on the man who opened a massive set of double doors with casual ease. She noted, irrelevantly again, that he wore wingtips today. This look suited him, much more than the down-home casual he'd tried to pull off…yesterday…when he'd asked her to marry him and she said yes.

That thought snapped her out of the sexual haze she'd fallen into.

"You're on time," he said lightly as she walked past him into his office suite. "I love that you're on time."

She shook her head because being near him, hearing him talk in that hypnotic voice…it was weakening her resolve. To do the right thing. To end this farce, once and for all. Because she had to.

She couldn't marry him.

Anya didn't think, she reached into her backpack, extracted the check kept in a secure compartment and held it out with shaking hands. "Here. Take this. Please."

His hand closed around her hand and she felt the contact down to her toes. It singed her. She wanted to jerk her hand away but that would make him *aware.*

It was the last thing she wanted. For him to be aware of her weaknesses and reactions.

Anya forced herself to stand still and keep her breathing even.

"What is it?"

She gently slid her hand out from under his. "It's a check for twelve thousand dollars. I know I'm about ten thousand short. But I'll pay every cent of it back. I promise."

Drake blinked. Slow and measured.

Anya's heart thudded loudly. The gesture a lot like a snake blinking before it struck on unsuspecting prey. She thrust it out again, almost hitting him in the chest with her haste.

"Please," she whispered. "Take the money."

"Why?"

"Because, it's the right thing for me to do. I can't be in debt to you."

"You're not." He examined the check she'd crumpled between them. "I never asked for the money back, did I?"

"No," she hurled back. "You wanted me to mar…" She snapped her mouth shut. Because saying the words out loud terrified her. Her migraine threatened to explode the insides of her brain to mush.

Drake gave her an appraising look from hooded lashes.

This close, she could smell his unique scent. Some fancy woodsy cologne that hid his sweaty stink. Although, she was close enough to see the lack of pit stains on his finely tailored shirt. Her knees buckled, just a little, when she breathed in more of his woodsy, masculine scent.

She locked them together, snapped her spine straighter and stared up at him. "Just take the money and consider us even. Okay?"

Drake chuckled. He actually chuckled. A rich, amused sound.

It sounded a little like the ticking of a bomb to Anya's hypersensitive ears.

"You know, I had a hunch you were one of those honest-to-their-toes kinds of people. And this pretty much proves it." He tapped the check. "Can you afford to give me this money, Anya?"

The way he said her name, drawing the two syllables out in sibilance, wrapped around her womb. Pulled her down to her basest need, in her heavy breasts. Her aching head danced with visions she was appalled of. Made her want to do even more unthinkable things, like pull him closer and kiss her name from his mouth.

She'd become unhinged.

"It doesn't matter whether I can afford this or not, Mr. Fallahil. It's the right thing to do for us honest-to-their-toes people." She managed to sound calm even though her body was going to war on her.

"That is very sweet of you, Anya. Thank you." He pocketed the check with the same careless grace he'd handled the whiskey tumbler.

She felt a trickle of relief at the gesture.

"So, that's it, then? We're done? I can go, right?"

He cocked his head again. "I don't understand. What are you on about?"

She tried to keep from licking her lips. "I gave you the money I owe you and now we have no further business with each other. Right?"

"Are you asking me or telling me?" He was so quiet, so watchful. It unnerved her.

"I'm …not going to marry you." Anya forced herself to move away from him. "I have thought it over and I can only conclude you're playing some kind of prank at my expense…getting your rocks off. And it's funny, haha." She gave a cackle. "But I am not going to marry you. Even as a prank. Not even for the most incredible work opportunity."

Somehow, in the course of her firm speech she'd come to a stop against his desk. She put one hand on it to steady herself.

"Is that it now?"

Anya nodded wildly. "YES! This is medieval. This kind of arrangement. And I have more pride and self-worth than just…"

"Saying yes to the deal of a lifetime?" He asked silkily.

He hadn't moved an inch. There was an ocean of distance between them but Anya felt cornered. Hunted.

She knew then, that coming here had been a mistake. A huge mistake.

"You caught me at a low moment," she admitted in a low voice.

Unable to look away from him. Unable to breathe, for looking at the little patch of skin visible through the opened top button of his impeccable shirt.

"And I wasn't thinking straight. And now that I am, of course, this is a terrible idea. Even if it were true, which it isn't!" Her voice rose in pitch. "So there you go. Yeah, this isn't happening."

Drake said nothing for a long moment. Then, in precise, almost poetic movements, he removed the check from his pocket, folded it into two and tore the two halves.

~~~~~~
~~~~~~

Panic made her voice rise. "What are you…?"

"No." His voice cut through her panic. It was so calm, but it held the violence of storms. "Fuck. No."

The pieces of the check fluttered to the floor between them.

Anya watched them go down in slow motion. When she looked up, there he was. Right in front of her.

Colossus rising, fury and thunder riding in the depths of his eyes, a single muscle ticking on his jaw an indicator that he wasn't in control even though he looked so calm.

So very calm.

"When you get to know me better you'll understand this better but, for now, let me just make this very, very clear, Anya. I never make deals I don't intend on following through."

His hand came forward and she sucked in an agonized breath, knowing her eyes were round with distress and utter panic. His fingers slid past her thigh to a sheaf of papers on the desk blotter.

"You gave me your word. I expect you to keep it. Same as me." He handed the papers to her. "That's our pre-nuptial agreement complete with an airtight NDA, spelling everything out in explicit detail. Please, sign it."

The words swam in front of Anya's blurry eyes. She looked up at him, still so close, too close for comfort.

The universe clashed within her. The very idea of being bonded to this man for any length of time, the mere thought of it so tantalizing in a terrifying way…it unsettled her even more.

She couldn't, not even at her most fundamental level, *want* what he was offering.

"But what about my right to refuse? And I gave you part of the money in good faith," she argued.

"You owe me the principle plus interest at, let's say eight percent. So that's twenty three thousand seven hundred and sixty dollars. And when you try to give me the next check, I'll buy controlling interest in this bank and shut it down."

Her mouth dropped open in unattractive shock. "You wouldn't."

He nodded coolly, a colossus in action. "I would. Just because I can."

"Why *me?* I'm…no one."

"You're perfect for my requirements," Drake shot back. "And I've looked into your background. Your credentials are, to say the least, impressive, Anya."

Anya flushed. *Did he know about Isqhi?* Had his security figured out her greatest secret? Then, common sense kicked in and she fought the panic down. If he'd found out about Ishqi, he'd be using her sister's incarceration as leverage to control her. But he hadn't…

"I don't even like you," she muttered.

He shrugged. "Liking me is not part of the requirement."

Anya couldn't help it. All of the tension broke in her, and one hot tear rolled down her cheek. She wiped it off angrily. "I've never like someone who manipulates people for their own amusement."

"I don't manipulate anyone, Anya."

"I don't believe you."

The statement made him react. He jerked her to her feet with a hand on the collar of her blazer. She hung on her toes between his legs, clutching at his immovable wrist.

"Let me go." She tried to twist away and was appalled to find his hold unbreakable. Her nails dug into his wrist.

More tears filled her eyes when he let her go as suddenly as he'd caught her. But she was damned if she'd give him the satisfaction of seeing her break.

Drake turned away, hands clenched, head bowed. "I'm sorry about that, Anya. That was unpardonable."

"Please," she tried again. "Please, don't do this to me. Please, Drake." Saying his name felt so intimate, almost as if she wanted to. And she didn't. *She didn't!*

He shook his head. "I can't. It's too late for that, Anya." He took what seemed to her a ragged breath. "If it's any consolation, you only have to tolerate me for three months. We'll both be free then."

"You really are going to go through with this, aren't you?" Anya was amazed at how calm she was. How in control.

Even though her life was in pieces and all because of the actions of this immoral, terrible man.

"I have to," he muttered. He still wouldn't look at her.

Who in their right mind would threaten to buy a goddamn bank and threaten to put it out of business just to get their own way? An unconscionable man.

The knowledge freed her from the spell she'd fallen into. Crystalized her anger and loathing, gave her the courage to do what needed to be done. Because she couldn't, in all good conscience, allow hundreds of people to suffer because of her own stupidity.

"I didn't think there was anything a man like you has to do." She reached for a pen on the blotter and started signing the papers blindly. Boldly. "But I want you to know this, Drake."

She finished signing and initialing all the papers. Gently stacked them in order.

Anya stepped away from the desk and picked up her backpack. She wore the straps with dignity. "I'm going to make you the worst wife on the planet."

He turned around then. And gave her yet another inscrutable look. "I look forward to it."

Anya tapped the papers on his desk. "I signed them. I trust you'll treat me fairly. And," a little devil made her add coolly, "If there is no clause in there for no sex or touching or anything of that sort, I suggest you call your people and add it right now."

"Is that so?"

She nodded rapidly. "I might be forced to do your bidding but I'm not going to make it easy for you."

"No," he agreed gravely. "That will make it very hard for me."

I will not blush, she swore to herself while she stared down the powerful man in her orbit. *I will not blush for him.*

"Have it your way." He nodded briskly. "I won't touch you without your consent."

"Or ever," she prompted.

"Or ever."

"Is that it or…?"

"I did want to have dinner with you. Maybe if we broke bread together, we could come to some sort of truce." Drake gave her a lopsided smile that would have hooked at her heart if she hadn't hardened it against him.

"No," she said. "There won't be any truce between us. We're at war, Mr. Fallahil."

He inclined his head. "War it is then. And may the best man win."

FOURTEEN

"It's not easy being a man like you, is it?" Robert Chan commented the next morning as he signed the last stack of papers Drake's lawyers presented him in the privacy of his own office in mid-town Hong Kong.

Chan Holdings were primarily based in Hong Kong so Drake had no choice but to expedite the trip along with his team. It had taken a fair bit of juggling but he'd managed an overnight charter and showed up on the dot of ten for this meeting.

He gave a small non-committal smile that absolutely did not reach his eyes. But the phrase stung.

A man like him. Who was a man like him? Why did everyone, Aster, Robert, *her* refer to him as some kind of a generality? When he'd done everything possible to ensure he was all there was.

Singular. Exceptional.

Alone.

"It's never easy being ourselves," he murmured. He looked for confirmation from his lawyers and Mili, who doubled up as legal counsel when he needed indemnity on certain deals. She was, after all, a Yale product.

Mili nodded infinitesimally so everything was kosher.

"But it's harder being anything other than ourselves," Drake finished, snapping the monogrammed folder containing the documents shut.

He handed it to Mili and she took it silently. The white bandage he'd wrapped around his busted knuckles gleamed dully.

The pain from wrecking his punching bag was welcome, familiar. And he used it to anchor himself when half of him was stuck back in that moment he'd grabbed a defenseless defiant woman just because he could. He'd spent the time he'd allocated for dinner with Anya working his penance out on the punching bag.

His team of fifteen upper management that he'd culled from the core team back on Sand Hill Road left the room as quietly as they'd come.

Their job, so to speak, was done.

Finally, it was just Drake and Robert in the room. He wrestled his focus back to the room with effort.

~~~~~~

Drake stood up, towering over Robert's six foot height. "It's been a pleasure doing business with you, Robert."

Robert, an almost-spitting male version of Aster with the same high-drawn brows and swept back inky black
~~~~~~

hair, looked at him appraisingly. "I'm glad you see it that way, Drake." His preppy accent showed in the way he said his 'Ts'.

"And why is that?"

"Because, my foolish daughter was willing to bring you into the family and that…would have been difficult for us," Robert ended diffidently.

"Difficult?" Drake cocked his head as if he was amused.

"Family's…everything for us in this part of the world, Mr. Fallahil. Where you come from and where you belong. And you--" Robert gave him another appraising look. Taking in the black Brioni suit with the matching waistcoat and wine-red shirt and tie that should have clashed with the black but oddly enhanced his ridiculous good looks. "You don't really belong here, do you?"

"Oh, I wouldn't say that, Mr. Chan," Drake said lightly. "I'm planning on making my mark here for decades to come."

"Yes, but that's just business. Anyone with deep enough pockets could achieve that. I mean *you,* Drake. You don't belong here," Robert said softly. "You don't belong anywhere because you refuse to."

Because the man's words hit uncomfortably close to home, Drake gave him another wide smile. "For now, my money belongs to you, Robert. So you can get ready for that expansion you've been wanting to get on with for the last five years. That should buy me enough street cred for at least a few years, shouldn't it?"

"It does and I'm grateful for it, Drake." Robert patted Drake's hand before letting it go. "Please don't misunderstand me. I just…didn't want to see my daughter's heart broken. So, I'm glad you took my suggestion under advisement and looked elsewhere for your bride. It's a, as you say Americans like to say, win-win for us all."

Robert smiled too. All teeth and a little heart because the poor bastard believed he'd gotten his way.

And maybe he had, Drake conceded as he looked at the older man.

Maybe if Robert Chan hadn't pressured Drake into finding a bride – both to keep his daughter at bay and to show good faith with the other members of his board – Drake wouldn't have done something so out of character as to force Anya Mallya-Bhatt to be his bride.

Maybe she wouldn't have declared war on him with eyes as brave as Boadicea.

Maybe he'd stop thinking about her.

"Yes," Drake agreed gravely. "It is a win-win."

Except he knew the ugly truth. They'd all lost in this game they were playing. Aster had won her father's regard but lost Drake. Robert had gained a business partner with seriously deep pockets but lost his daughter's love.

And he, Drake…well, he'd made billions in a deal that should not have happened in the first place so he supposed all he lost was his pride at having been brought low by the Chans, in their own way.

Pride, Drake had discovered when he was nothing but a terrified boy, was not the end of the world. Heart was. He'd lost his a long time ago.

So, it didn't matter what the Chans – father and daughter – thought of him. He was beyond them in every way that mattered.

"Stay," Robert invited him. "Have lunch with me and the other partners. They're eager to talk expansion plans with you."

"I'd love to," Drake said. "But I have an important call I can't miss at all. So can I rain check?"

Robert nodded, genially. "Of course. Nothing keeps you away from business, does it?"

"Sure."

~ ~ ~ ~ ~

Drake exited Robert's office and found Mili waiting for him by the elevator banks. Today, she wore flowing pants and a lacy shell under a mannish blazer that emphasized her long, Thoroughbred lines.

She tapped her air-buds and ended the call she was on, mid-way. "You paid sixteen percent more than you had to, to get your seat on the Chan's Board."

"I know." Drake gave her a droll glance. "Teach."

Mili rolled her eyes in a thoroughly unprofessional gesture. "You'd only do that if you knew for certain that, eventually, you're going to take over the Board and make it work for you, one hundred percent."

"And how well you know me, Mils," he commented. "Two years," he predicted. "In two years, Aster will take over as MD or Chairman, with my help, of course. And then the expansion plans will become a lot more green and energy-efficient than they are right now."

"And they say you don't have a heart, Fallahil."

He shrugged. "I don't."

Mili shook her head. "One of these days…" she murmured.

"Is it time, yet?" Drake cut short her wordless praise.

Mili looked at the clock on her phone. "Almost. Bret should be done with homework by now."

"Awesome. Is the connection good inside the elevator?"

The doors dinged open on command.

"I don't know. Why don't you finish the call in that alcove," she pointed to a cozy little space off the elevator banks, "and then come and find me downstairs?"

"Sure."

Mili almost got into the elevator when she hesitated, took a deep breath and turned around. "Are you going to tell Lily about…you know, your impending marriage?"

Drake shook his head instantly. "Why would I do that? It's got nothing to do with her?"

Mili opened her mouth as if to say something else but then thought better of it. She simply nodded. "I'll wait for you downstairs. With your bubble tea."

Drake blew her a kiss and waited for her to catch it. She did, as was customary between them. But he also detected acute disappointment in her normally blank eyes and that surprised him.

"Listen, I know its short notice but would you? Take care of the details?"

"What details?" Mili asked.

"You know. The Mallya-Bhatt details." He waved his hand as if to encompass everything.

Mili's nod was a long time coming but it finally came. "Sure thing, Sir. Consider it done."

The elevator doors closed on her cool, reproving expression.

Then he dismissed it, and her, from his mind, walked swiftly to the alcove for the best and most important part of his week.

Talking to his nephew.

~~~~~

"...And so I've decided to concentrate on dribbling because Kit says that's the most important part of playing basketball anyway."
~~~~~

"Is that so, buddy?" Drake smiled as he held the phone in both hands so he could see Bret's dribbling. "That's some epic dribbling, Bret."

Bret smiled. A happy, well-adjusted pre-teen who'd somehow emerged unscathed from everything that had ever happened to him.

From the fact of his birth, to his mother's sudden move to Chicago when he'd finally bought the beach mansion on Malibu for Lily and Bret and then…meeting the Subramanians, Bret's dead father's family.

"We have to have a pick-up game when you come for Christmas."

"It's a deal," Drake replied solemnly. "It would be my pleasure to kick your ass shooting hoops, my son."

Bret grinned. "That's what Kit says too. But he never does."

Drake struggled to keep the delight on his face but he was pissed off. Or more accurately, he was resigned. Because Kit Barranos, that built motherfucker who loved his sister, was here to stay.

And he was, unfortunately, not afraid of Drake's size or his power.

Oddly, Drake did respect him for it. He just didn't have to like it. *Fuck.*

"You're thinking of a curse word," Bret guessed accurately. He bounced the ball casually on his knees, already taller than Drake had seen him six months ago.

During a truly disastrous Christmas reunion with Lily.

"How do you know that?"

"It's how Kit looks when mom talks about you," Bret imparted confidentially.

Drake's corresponding smile was broad and genuine. "Your mom does love to talk me up, doesn't she?"

"She loves you, Uncle Drake. We both do," Bret spoke without a trace of artifice. He touched the screen with his bony hand.

He looked so like Lily had when she was twelve, right then.

His hair was a mix of dark and blond and his eyes were dark and solemn, which did nothing to detract from his boyish beauty, chipped tooth and all.

No, Drake realized with a start. Bret looked like *him.* When he'd been twelve. A lot more mature than any twelve year old boy should ideally be.

"I love you right back, sweetheart," Drake murmured roughly. He touched the screen too, and he was surprised to see his fingers trembled the slightest. "You're my favorite kid of all."

Bret grinned. "That's because I'm the only kid you have."

"This cannot be denied."

And it was true. Bret was Drake's heir, along with Lily, inheriting every single asset Drake ever owned, in the event if anything happened to Drake.

With an inner shudder, Drake realized he'd have to add Anya as a dependent on his will now. Even if it was only for three short months.

What had he *done?*

"Are you okay, Uncle Drake?" Bret asked curiously, seeing the frown bisect Drake's forehead.

Drake shook off his misgivings. "I'm fine, buddy. Tell me more about school stuff. Are you doing those extra math problems I sent you last week?"

"I am. Although mom gets really mad when she can't crack them. So we talk to Uncle Dev or Auntie Zara, whoever's online."

Drake nodded. "That's great, buddy. Always ask for help when you need to."

"Mom's calling for me. Should I tell her you're here? Do you want to talk to her?"

Drake hesitated briefly. The urge to talk to his baby sister, his Lily girl, was strong. Mostly because Bret had set off a small explosion in him with his unguarded confession of love and family.

And because he *missed* Lily sometimes so intensely it was a physical ache.

But, Lily knew him. She knew him as well as Mili did. And if Mili could detect ambivalence in him over the upcoming nuptials then he wouldn't be able to keep it from Lily. And Lily wasn't his employee.

She wouldn't keep her mouth shut like Mili had, just now.

So, he shook his head. "Sorry, bud. Not now. I have to go back to work. But I'll check in with you guys, next week, okay? Promise."

"Nah, make a deal with me, Uncle Drake. You never welch on a deal."

"I might have raised you wrong, kid." Drake shook his head in fond amusement. "But fine. Deal. I'll talk to your mom next week."

"Bye, Uncle Drake." Bret threw the ball at the screen and Drake made to catch it. The screen went blank as the call ended.

He touched the blank screen once more. Still smiling fondly.

If there was one thing he was absolutely glad to have won in this life, it was his nephew's heart and smile. The most priceless thing in the world to him.

~~~~~~

The phone vibrated again, indicating a private number. He picked it up without checking info.

"Drake Fallahil here."
~~~~~~

"Hello, son," the caller responded. "Long time, no see." The voice was raspy, with age and the effects of imbibing copious amounts of Kentucky's finest moonshine.

Drake's blood ran cold. His spine snapped erect and all happy thoughts fled from his brain, leaving him empty and drained. He licked his lips. "What do you want?"

"To see you, son, of course."

Drake shook his head. Then remembered *he* couldn't see him. "That's not possible. I'm not in the States."

"That's fine. I can come to you. Can't I?" The raspy voice taunted him with perfect innocence.

Drake remembered the kiss of leather on his skin. The burn and sting of it. As he hunched and curled within himself, trying to make himself invisible. To completely disappear.

"No," Drake answered coldly. "You can't. Whatever you need, send me the information. I'll get it done."

"I don't want…"

"Yes, you do," Drake countered icily. "That's all you do. Want. And I'm okay with it. I owe you that. Now I have to go. Email me your list…" He made himself say the next word. "Dad."

Then he disconnected the call while the voice rasped on and he heard not a thing.

Drake carefully inserted the phone in his jacket pocket. His hands wanted to shake, badly, they wanted to give vent to the monster coiling up. Crush the phone into tiny pieces or beat someone bloody.

It would be satisfying. At least as satisfying as crushing the windpipe of his father with his own two hands which is what he really wanted.

This man was responsible for the way his fate cards had played out and Drake couldn't forget it for a second. He'd abandoned his mother when she was pregnant with him and left her at the mercy of an inhuman beast who would have surely killed him if he could have.

His chest cavity felt hollow as if someone had reached inside his rib cage and grabbed everything worthwhile while he still lived. If he let himself, he could feel the lashes on his back throbbing again.

His eyes were dry, but they burned. As if he'd stared into the bright sun too long.

Drake closed them.

Anya Mallya-Bhatt's Boadicea eyes swam into his head. The way she'd looked at him, while he grabbed her by the throat and hung her suspended in the air. A low point for him, when he prided himself on his indomitable control.

His fists unclenched, finger by finger. His breath returned to normal and he could think again. He was in control again.

Everything was fine, Drake assured himself as he walked to the elevators. Punched in a button with more force than necessary.

He had everything he could ever want, with this new deal. And nothing, not even his thrice-damned father, could ruin it for him.

The miracle of it was, he actually believed his own words.

FIFTEEN

Two incredibly short days later, Anya looked at herself in the free-standing floor-length mirror in the impersonal hotel room of The Marina Bay Sands Hotel. Behind her was a huge acres-large bed raised on a dais she wouldn't be able to navigate with the silver, strappy heels she wore.

"My baby is so beautiful," Swati said, as she came to a stop behind Anya. "A beautiful bride."

Anya wore a bridal georgette sari, in vermillion red with a golden zari border. Her blouse was a sweet three-fourths sleeve design that covered her modestly, except when she walked. Then the leaf-shaped design gaped open like two halves of a whole at the back.

It was understated and sexy… perfect.

Anya was secretly impressed that the designer had gotten her measurements so accurately without actually fitting her out.

The vanity lady who'd done her hair and makeup an hour ago had marveled over her hair and preferred to leave it to curl to its own devices. Just expertly applying a holding cream so the curls maintained their shape and shone with luster. She'd twisted two thick strands from the front and created a sort of crown braid tucked with exotic tiny rosebuds which smelled divine.

Her makeup enhanced her golden looks – the bronzer highlighting her cheeks and the lightly dusted golden eye shadow and black liner creating an arch of her brows that did not previously exist.

The aesthetician had asked her if she needed to be waxed *down there*, for maintenance. Anya had blushed and said no.

She was not going to maim herself for a man who would never see her naked. Nope.

Anya wore no jewelry, except a pair of simple swan-shaped gold studs in her ears. But the shoes, oh…the shoes were divine. Silver, strappy with diamante studs for buckles; they shone with the brightness of a falling star.

The shoes were the fanciest thing she'd ever worn in her life. They made her feel powerful and sexy when she slipped into them.

Like Anya, Swati too wore a simple sari. Hers was a deep wine-red that perfectly set off her complexion while enhancing her looks, with a blouse that cinched at her waist. Her hair was done up in a simple French chignon tucked with an ornate golden pin. At her waist was a shimmering gold belt – a *kamarpatta* – as it was called.

All provided by Drake freaking Fallahil and his preternaturally efficient assistant, Mili Iyer.

She'd not seen him since that fateful encounter two nights ago. One she still sweated bullets over.

But, true to his word, *things* had started arriving the morning after she woke up from the world's worst migraine.

First, had come the bridal outfits. Then, the accessories to go with it. And finally, a fancy smartphone that wasn't even in the market (she'd looked it up) had showed up.

When she'd inserted her OG SIM card in it, the first text had popped up.

Thanks for agreeing to marry my beastly boss. You saved my job! – Mili.

Anya couldn't help but giggle at that off-color and very imperious comment from the assistant. She'd responded with a cheeky emoji. It set the tone for their correspondence.

Mili had made what was, at heart, a very awkward and embarrassing process, fun. She'd sent cute texts and even cuter GIFs with each new parcel, making sure to poke fun at her beastly boss every chance she got.

And Mili, bless her heart, did not for one second make Anya feel like a woman shilling on Seventh Street because she'd agreed to this farce of a marriage for her own reasons. So, Anya had confided in her about her mother's failing health and the lack of a surgeon's appointment.

Mili was so nice about it, understanding and sympathetic without turning it into a pity party that Anya wanted to confide in her some more. Tell her about her difficulties with Ishqi and the real reason she was trapped in this horrible arrangement.

But Anya couldn't forget the most important detail of all.

She'd never given Drake her address. She'd never told him anything about herself. But the packages – both hers and her mother's - arrived at the correct address and were the actual size, suitable to their complexions, right down to the damn shoe size.

He'd figured everything out about her, or, more likely, made Mili figure it all out.

She couldn't trust anyone. Not even the woman who had the gall to defy Drake.

And now here she was.

About to join herself in unholy matrimony with a man she knew less than nothing about.

"So beautiful," Swati sniffed, inelegantly. She placed her chin on her daughter's shoulder.

The mirror reflected the two of them back in the blinding sunlight – a beautifully-dressed mother and daughter. No one could mistake them for anything else.

Anya felt a bittersweet pang at the gesture. Swati had lost weight in the last few months, since the pain in her knees became untenable, and now she was light as a bird.

"You are, mama," Anya said softly. "You are so beautiful."

Swati squeezed her shoulder and hugged her close. "I'm so glad you have someone to take care of you, Anya. You deserve it."

Anya nodded. "You take care of me, mama."

Swati shook her head, her cheek brushing against Anya's carefully made up jaw. "No, *beta*. I haven't. Between my job and raising Ishqi, I left you alone far too much. But your sister, she's so special. I worried so much about her. I'm so happy I don't have to worry about you anymore."

Anya felt a hot lump take hold of her throat, ready to spew out in great big sobs. Of disappointment and unending grief.

How could her mother be so fucking *blind?* Couldn't she see Anya was in ruins?

Because her mother was *happy.* She was thrilled. She thought this was a love match. A shotgun love match but something Anya was willingly choosing, with a son-in-law she'd yet to meet.

Especially, when Anya had explained who Drake was and showed her some of the profiles done on him online Swati'd been amazed. Freaked out. Flat out delighted.

She'd somehow been deluded into thinking Anya had caught the attention of the man who'd won Richest Man of The World award on Harun's HNI list. He'd liked

Anya enough to somehow fall so hard for her, a complete nobody, he wanted to make it official!

Anya would have laughed hysterically if she wasn't afraid those laughs would turn into never-ending tears.

So she'd allowed her mom to keep her delusions, and played along with her.

It was easy enough to do when the *things* started arriving. And when Mili turned out to be such a thorough and sweet conspirator.

She'd gotten through the last two days on copious amounts of caffeine, ibuprofen for her migraine and sheer nerves.

Now, though, the moment of reckoning was near.

It was here.

Now, she had to step out of this fancy hotel room with its million-dollar view and sign her name to a piece of paper that would legally and irrevocably bind her to a man she despised.

And she did despise him, Anya promised herself. She despised him and everything he stood for. All that wealth and power, all that attention and casual displays of dominance. All of it, she hated.

And she hated, most of all that it didn't seem to matter to him at all.

He genuinely did not care what she thought of him. How much she detested him. His feelings did not enter the equation at all. And so, by consequence, hers were dismissed too.

Every time she closed her eyes, she could feel him yank her to her toes with one hand on her blazer. She could see every line on his wretchedly handsome face, so close she could have touched him if she wanted. And she could see the dead quiet in his eyes as he handled so cruelly.

She could see the coiled violence in him, like a living thing. And she would have welcomed fighting it.

And every time, *every* time, she did something. *Anything.* Than stand there helpless and broken in his arms.

She slapped him. Scratched those stunning eyes out. Headbutted him. Kneed him in the balls.

She took action. She wasn't some passive doll he could manipulate to his will.

But she hadn't done anything when she could have. So now here she was. This was her price to pay for being helpless and broken for a single moment.

The doors to the entirely white suite opened and he walked in.

The man who seemed to feel nothing for her.

~ ~ ~ ~ ~

Anya forgot to breathe.

She could only watch as Drake swept into the room. He wore his customary outfit – a well-fitting, bespoke suit. This one was a shade of blue so dark it was almost black. But his shirt was a blinding white and his tie was the same color as her sari. So, he'd actually coordinated his outfit with hers.

Or, Anya thought prosaically, Mili had done the deed for him.

His hair was shorn at his nape so the waves didn't fall past his collar. But she'd not imagined the brutal power of his eyes or the way watching him watch her in the mirror twisted something sharp and sensational deep inside her.

Anya deliberately took her eyes off him in the mirror and focused on getting the single pleat of her sari draped just so.

"Ohh. Drake. Mr. Fallahil. You're here," Swati fluttered about. Her face awash with delight and pleasant consternation.

Drake stopped and actually hugged her mother. His arms large and strangely comforting. "Mrs. Bhatt, it's an honor to meet you," he said somberly. "I'm so sorry I couldn't meet you sooner and pay my regards. But work's been insane this week."

"Mr. Fallahil, please." She put a hand to her throat. "It's perfectly alright."

"Call me Drake, please. I'd love it," he invited.

Swati's eyes widened. "Me too," she smiled tremulously.

Drake inclined his head. He placed a long velvet case he extracted from his jacket pocket in Swati's palm. "This is for you."

"You didn't have to, Drake." But she opened the case anyway, eyes shining bright with anticipation.

Anya had to watch and suffer as her mother gasped at the simple diamond chain Drake helped fasten at her throat. She had to watch her mother be charmed into submission by the man soon to be her son-in-law.

And if that something sharp twisted tighter in her, until it felt like she was bleeding, she told herself it was okay.

It was okay because her mom looked happy. And when was the last time she'd worn a bauble so shiny and pretty?

Drake murmured something to Swati. Swati gave Anya a knowing smile and left the room after patting Drake's cheek.

Leaving Anya alone with her would-be groom.

~ ~ ~ ~ ~ ~

Before Drake could straighten from his half-crouch, Anya turned around and hurled hot words at him. "I'm returning all of this back to you the second this madness is over."

He raised his brow. "I'm glad to hear that. Thank you." He watched the closed door for a silent, charged moment. "She doesn't look like she is in pain, does she? Her gait hasn't changed."

All of Anya's anger drained out as she tried to process his words. "What? What did you just say?" She asked stupidly.

"Your mother." He walked over to her. "I know she needs a knee replacement in both knees. That she suffers from acute rheumatoid arthritis. I know you've been trying to get her in to see Dr. Prabhu at Singapore Memorial for the last three months and your insurance doesn't cover the cost of the surgery. You can't afford for her to have the surgery, can you?"

Anya's breath returned in a massive rush. One of relief and indignation at having her failures spelled out so casually by this man.

"Well." She patted her sari pleat in place needlessly. "You have done your homework on me. I wonder what else you know about me, Mr. Fallahil."

"I know that your mother migrated her from Mangalore more than thirty years ago with her husband. She was a teacher in a high school and he was a banker. He died soon after they came here, a heart attack, I believe. And she's done whatever she could to raise you here, ever since," he finished softly.

"She cleaned houses," Anya said bitterly, the shame of it stinging her until everything good turned ugly. Dirty. "On Great Albert Road and Orchard Street and Jurong Park. On her hands and knees until they gave out. She didn't have a formal teaching degree in India and it was too expensive to get one here and between raising I..I am talking too much," she ended abruptly.

Drake raised one hand, as if to touch her. She could see the two blood-red buttons, monogrammed with his initials DF in the mirror.

He didn't. Instead, he extracted something from his pocket.

One was a paper of some sort, the other was a dazzling sapphire in the shape of a teardrop suspended from an almost invisible chain. The damn thing could be a twin for the color of his eyes – a wild, echoing blue.

"I'm not wearing that," Anya said instantly.

Panic and something else, something awfully like longing filled her heart. At the idea of allowing him to give her something so infinitely precious and *beautiful.*

He handed her the paper.

Her breath shortened as she read through it. She raised bludgeoned eyes to his when she read it a second, third time. "This is a hospital intake bill."

"It is. Her surgery's been scheduled for tomorrow. We have to get done with the ceremony in an hour, because

Dr. Prabhu's going to see her at two pm sharp. And you'd want to be there for the consult, I know."

Anya's lips parted. "Why…"

Drake shrugged, gave her a tiny smile. It actually reached his eyes, although it didn't light them up. So she knew he didn't *really* mean it. "It's customary for couples to give each other wedding gifts, isn't it? And this is the one thing you want more than anything else in the world."

Anya gulped. "It is." She clutched the bill and crushed in nerveless fingers. "It is, Drake. Thank you so much. I can't…I can't." She shook her swimming head. She looked up at him with utter, guileless gratitude. "*Thank you.* I won't forget what you've done for me."

He nodded. "I like to keep all my employees happy so they produce optimally." The words were business-like, so was his tone.

She would have believed him but she saw the way his eyes lingered on her neck. A slow fire licked at the edges of his expression.

As if he couldn't help himself.

Anya nodded, slower than him. "Truce?" She took the necklace without him offering it to her.

"You'd like to call a truce?"

"I have to now, don't I? You've given me the only thing I want in the whole world. I can't be mad at you after that." Anya swept her hair to one side and tried to attach the open loop to the eye.

"May I?" He spoke formally.

She nodded.

Drake brushed even more of her hair over her shoulder. His touch was light, the pads of his callused fingers mindful of her skin. She still felt chills run up and down her arms, her back, even the tips of her toes.

He bent low, his tongue poking out between his teeth as he focused on getting the delicate loop to open. His hands touched her nape, disturbing the tiny baby hairs over there, fluttering soft things to life that joined the sharp thing twisting inside her.

Making her forget herself, swept away by the sheer kindness of his gesture.

It would be so easy, too easy, to lean against him. Give him more of her weight, and have him bear all of the many burdens she carried. His broad shoulders certainly could carry them, much better than her.

Anya watched his expression with fascination. He looked absorbed in the task. His nose a sharp, pointed, breathy line against her sensitive back.

Finally, the loop slid closed and the jewel hung between her breasts. A fat pendulum that seemed to be held up by her chest, defying gravity.

Drake stepped back immediately.

"What's this for then?" Anya asked him, touching the jewel. Aware, exactly, where her hand rested.

Right between her breasts. Knowing his eyes followed the line of her hand.

His eyes hooded, turned liminal. "That's for me. Your gift to me is your acquiescence, Anya." He smiled slow, sure. Vulturine. "And I thank you for your gift."

Anya nodded. Tight and coiled. Ready to strike the man who'd taken something so pure and beautiful and mangled it to destruction. "You're welcome."

"Shall we walk out, then?" He offered her his arm.

"I prefer walking to the gallows without your help," she replied with what dignity remained. "So, thanks. But no thanks."

SIXTEEN

Anya's wedding day passed in a blur. In later days, if someone had asked her to describe her wedding – the moments leading up to it – she would have been hard-pressed to answer them.

The wedding itself took a brisk five minutes, in a lounge overlooking the infinity pool at MBS. A celebrant presided over a formal ring-exchanging ceremony, where Drake swiftly, impersonally slid a thick gold band over her left ring finger. They signed a legal document the celebrant had brought, her name above his.

And that was it.

Mili, the sole groom's guest took a picture with her fancy phone camera to procure the wedding certificate.

Swati wiped streaming eyes and embraced Mili and Anya and Drake, a second time.

The groom declined champagne and ordered sparkling water for everyone, which he drank quickly. As if he was parched.

They'd not touched each other since he'd stepped back from her after placing that breathtaking sapphire around her neck.

Anya was in abject shock.

Both at the clinical precision with which the event was executed and Drake, *her husband's,* dismissive words just moments before.

He couldn't possibly have known how much her mom's surgery had meant to her. She'd only barely mentioned it to Mili and that too in a snarky text.

It was a little terrifying how he'd arranged for it… made the impossible possible. That he'd done it for his own nefarious reasons did not, for one second, take away from the enormity of the gesture.

So, Anya spent the second half of her wedding day in consult with the premier orthopedic surgeon in the country.

She kept her weepy feelings to herself and listened to the doctor list out the possible side effects of the surgery, all the pre-op tests they were going to begin on her mother. If all went as well as expected, then her mom's surgery would be scheduled for the following day.

She watched Swati being wheeled away into a private suite that cost more than their bank savings and thanked all the gods for this tiny miracle.

~~~~~

When her mom was wheeled back into her lushly appointed room, Anya had arranged for a small go-bag to be brought from their tiny apartment in Little India.
~~~~~

She'd changed out of her wedding finery into something hospital-appropriate.

Her usual attire of jeans and a sweatshirt, with no trace of makeup. Her hair pulled into a sleek tail.

Her mom smiled wanly when she saw Anya, curled on the plush wing chair, flipping through her Politics of Economics primer.

"What are you doing here, *beta*?"

"How are you? Did they poke you with too many needles? Are you hungry? You must be. I ordered some dal rice and a salad for you. They have a personal chef for patients here. I did not know that." Anya finished fussing with the one-thousand thread count Egyptian cotton sheets.

Swati caught Anya's fluttering hands between both of hers. "Go home, Anya. You don't have to stay here anymore."

Anya bit her lip. "But…"

"It's your wedding day. And your husband." Anya's heart jolted at hearing that phrase again. "Has done us an enormous kindness. Spend your first day as man and wife with him, Anya. He deserves it."

And that was the truly humiliating part.

He *did* deserve it.

Drake had done the most-husbandly thing ever, put her family first, and taken care of this medical crisis. And he'd done it without her having to ask for it. No matter how vile he was, this was an enormous kindness.

If she didn't know better, she'd think he cared about her well-being. But she also knew he didn't lie. So when he said he was thinking of his employee's productivity she believed him.

"But your surgery is tomorrow, mama."

Swati patted her hand again. "And you can come see me off before they take me in to the OT. But I can't, as your mother, allow you to spend your wedding night in the hospital with me."

Swati's expressive eyes filled with tears. "I should be preparing to bid you farewell. Help you pack your trousseau and send you to his place like a traditional Indian mother would, Anya."

"I don't want a traditional Indian mother, mama. I want you," Anya whispered fiercely.

"Ishqi should be here for you, at the very least."

Anya swallowed words of recrimination at the fragile longing in her mother's eyes. "She will be here soon enough. But she isn't here tonight, mama. And I can't possibly leave you here alone."

"You won't," Swati reassured her. "The nurses are so nice, Anya. They even watch the same soaps as I do. I'll be fine. Besides." She winked, her mom actually winked, at her for the first time ever. "I have a pretty good idea why my son-in-law rushed you into this wedding. Don't disappoint him because of me."

Anya bit back a wild laugh, made an inconsequential remark while feelings ran wild and unchecked inside her. She also knew this was a battle she'd lost. Her mom wanted her gone so she would go.

Anya gathered the duffel bag which contained her bridal finery and exited the hospital. She was surprised to see twilight barely falling over the sky.

Time had passed by so slowly when her whole world had changed for the better. It was amazing.

It was…Drake, she realized.

On an impulse she barely understood, she texted Mili from her brand-new phone.

What kind of cuisine does your beastly boss enjoy the most?

The answer came swiftly. *Down home American cookin'.*

Since Anya had absorbed enough pop culture to know what Mili meant, she flagged a cab to the nearest meat market, bought a delicious calf's hind, Idaho potatoes, and various greens.

Then, she did the bravest thing of all and took another cab to where she knew he lived.

An exclusive residential neighborhood in the most secure and picturesque place in the city. Gardens by the Bay.

~~~~~
~~~~~

Anya placed a hand on the cab's glass window and watched the three-hundred foot tall supertrees, lit up for the evening show, gleam in a rainbow of colors.

She was enchanted. In love.

The cab took a small rut-like road through the side entrance of the Gardens, keeping the supertrees in view the whole time. They arrived at a tall, imposing wrought-iron gate done up in thief's black.

A turbaned guard peeked in to the passenger side and saw Anya's face. "You're Mrs. Fallahil," he said, without any inflection.

Anya jolted inside, as if she'd touched a livewire. But she patted the brown grocery bags she'd laid so carefully on the seat next to her. As if they could give her courage.

"Yes," she said neutrally. "Yes, I am."

"Mr. Fallahil has sent your access pass, ma'am." The man handed her a white embossed keycard. "Please swipe this to access the atrium area."

Anya nodded, mystified.

The cab drove inside, through a winding road which seemed to have no destination. Into a wild, jungle-like paradise with flowers and trees of all kinds, some of them as tall as the super trees. But without the lights to keep them lit up.

Finally, a single, needle-like structure rose up through the jungle. It was made entirely of steel and concrete, with creepers clinging to one side of the structure, embracing it like a lover might. And, best of all, a super tree grew up right next to the structure, twinning it for breadth and beauty.

Anya stepped out, enchanted all over again.

She swiped her access pass at the locked and unguarded gate. Juggled her duffel bag and the four bags of groceries and walked through the church-quiet lobby. The same lush and verdant theme echoed through the masonried lobby.

Anya spied the elevator bank cleverly concealed behind an Assyrian Wall reproduction.

She swiped her card again and the elevator whisked her in a whoosh of speed and air to the atrium.

To where Drake's apartment was.

She had it on good authority that he was in meetings till nine so she had a good two hours till he came back. To a wedding feast worthy of its name.

~~~~~

Anya's first impression of Drake's penthouse was one of limitless space. Echoing, vast, limitless space. It too had glass walls on two sides, as if to invite the city right into the insides of the space. Even with the spectacular view of the Marina Bay and the best spots of the city, this apartment looked…alien.

Set apart from the world it inhabited.
~~~~~

Anya almost felt dizzy as she took in the view from the vast height she occupied. Then, she shook her head, and tried to locate the kitchen.

She'd dumped her stuff on what looked like an ornately carved back of a marble horse, or at least she hoped it was a horse. Maybe it was a unicorn.

The kitchen was a white, spotless, concealed space attached to the living space. She had to actually press a few buttons on a console to call up the hob, open the refrigerator door and the cabinets containing the pots and pans.

But, once she'd figured all of it out, she tucked her hair into a bun, cracked her hands and the cricks off her neck and got down to cooking. The activity soothed her nerves at moving into a strange man's apartment and using his kitchen to cook him a meal.

Pretty soon, the steaks were broiling, the potatoes were scrubbed and marinated with rosemary and cracked sea salt and pepper. She stuck everything into the oven according to the instructions in the online video she'd found on making simple American steak and potatoes.

Then she made the sauce Dianne which went best with steak, using fancy distilled vinegar flown in from France and pepper that were ground in Colombia.

The kitchen smelled of meat and veggies cooking so she left it all in the oven, before setting the table in the kitchen itself.

This wasn't a romantic dinner so Anya chose to forego candlelight tapers and stuck to the Murano blown-glass bulbs suspended from the draft ceiling. The plates were sturdy china she'd found in a cabinet. The wine was a bottle of red she'd found in the wine rack, right next to the refrigerator.

Soft classical music piped in from her new phone and she was pleased with the look she'd achieved.

Down home. American. Not even remotely suggestive of anything other than good food and gratitude.

"Well done, babe," she murmured to herself.

Then she shook her hair free of the bun, settled down to wait for Drake in the high back chair that came with the steel and glass square dining table.

She chose the Politics of Economics for some light reading. Pretty soon, she was so absorbed in highlighting the way some random Norwegian had spoken carelessly in a 1989 UN conclave and changed the course of global economic policy forever.

It was why she almost jumped out of her bones when she heard Drake growl, "What the fuck are you doing, Anya?"

~~~~~~

Anya brushed a curl of hair out of her eye and answered with a wave of her hand. "I was waiting for you, actually. For, you know, dinner." She tried a grateful smile at the bleary-eyed man in front of her.
~~~~~~

He still wore the suit he'd worn in the morning when he'd signed his name below hers and claimed her as his wife. Except now, the tie was tucked into his pocket.

She could see the tantalizing patch of skin between his chest and neck with a little whorl of hair poking out.

Heat filled her, making her lazy and languid.

Drake stared at her as if she'd grown horns. "Why would you do that?"

Anya blinked. Bit her lip. "I don't understand. Why would I do what? I thought…" She shook her head. "Was I mistaken in thinking you wanted me here?"

"Of course you have to be here if people have to buy this arrangement," he bit off impatiently. Rubbing his neck. "But, I wasn't…did you cook all this food?"

Anya nodded. "I did." She tried the smile again, even though it strained her facial muscles. "It's all your favorites. Steak and potatoes. Mili told me they're what you like best."

"Mili talks too fucking much," he muttered.

"I'm sorry," she said stiltedly. "I was just trying to thank you for what you've done for my mama. It means a lot to us and this is a small token of my gratitude--"

"Fuck your gratitude," he growled.

Anya stumbled back from the chair. It clattered to the floor. "I beg your pardon?"

He gave her a leisurely look. One that took in her holey sweatshirt, her bare unpainted face. The slim-fitting but chain store jeans. Her Frozen socks.

"I don't want or need your gratitude or anything else. And as for dinner, your CI, Mili forgot to inform you that I already had dinner with the Chengs. It was a celebratory meal."

He picked up the wine bottle. "And I'm going to continue celebrating with this excellent Pinot Noir." His eyes gleamed in the low lamplight like the very devil. He looked nothing like the charming man who'd been so incredibly sweet to her mother, just hours before.

"Care to join me, Anya?"

Her lips went numb at his cutting dismissal. But she knew her place now. So she shook her head very softly.

"No, no thank you. I'll leave you to your celebration."

She made to leave the kitchen when he called her name.

Anya turned around slowly and faced him.

It was a bit like seeing a living, breathing colossus. And he was just as distant and enigmatic as the mythical creature. He wasn't really hers in any concrete way which about shattered her heart.

"What?" She forced herself to ask with no break in her voice.

He picked up her textbook and tossed it to her. She caught it more by reflex than any real design. "Take your stuff with you."

Anya hugged her textbook to her chest, turned on her heel and fled the room.

It was only in the privacy of the guest room, with the door firmly bolted and shut that she slid down against it, still clutching the textbook and started sobbing. Slowly and quietly and no surcease.

It was how Anya Fallahil spent her wedding night. Crying till her heart seemed to break from the strain of it.

SEVENTEEN

Drake woke up a married man with an epic hangover.

His head pounded in a clash of inchoate cymbals and drums. It all beat a straight line down the center of his brain and his face, culminating on both sides of his jaw which also ached like the very devil.

He rotated his neck a couple of times to remove the kinks and then went to the bathroom located near the living room. It was a functional space, unlike the humongous thing on the other side of the atrium which could easily house a family of seven.

He looked exhausted, he noted as he peed. The mask of control, of invincibility was gone. He had bloodshot eyes from imbibing too much and the lines on his face felt embedded there.

He washed his hands once his business was done, scratching his exposed belly over the boxers he'd worn to the couch where he'd crashed once he'd finished okaying the memos for the next week.

Drake carefully avoided thinking at all, keeping up a mental chatter that consisted of future to-dos and ticking off past achievements. It worked, really well even, when he wore his robe and padded barefoot to the space in the living room he'd commandeered as his office.

His watch – the one designed with the same OS Bharat Shrinivasan had used to build his unhackable phone – beeped a message out.

7 am. Dan Houston, office complex consult.

He looked at his robe, then at the time. His stomach growled. Drake opted to feed his belly over looking presentable. He wandered to the kitchen, just as his tablet signaled an incoming video call.

He thumbed it to answer and the architect's affably handsome face filled the screen. He too had dark blonde hair and blue eyes. It was where the resemblance ended. Because Dan was all lightness and charm; it practically oozed out of him through the screen.

"Hello, Fallahil, you look positively chipper this fine morning." Dan was English. Pleasantly, faultlessly English. With the posh upper crust accent, pedigreed ancestry, and impeccable manners to go with it.

"Yeah, I had too much to drink last night, Houston. So fuck off." Drake pronounced Houston the way Dan had asked him to – as Howston instead of Hueston. It was a weird family thing, he'd proclaimed when Drake had asked him about it.

"Since when do you drink too much?" Dan asked cheerily, sipping his steaming mug of tea, like the Englishman he was.

Drake stopped dead as he saw the remains of the dinner Anya, *his wife,* had made for him last night. The neatly-covered white dishes accusing soldiers as proof of his perfidy.

And everything, every last bad feeling – of inadequacy, helplessness, and rage – came back to him.

He remembered, with the curse of his incredible memory, the words he'd snapped at her. Remembered the way she'd caught her textbook in trembling hands, a tiny waif who'd wandered into a monster's orbit.

But, most of all, most damning of all, he remembered the way *he'd* felt when he'd entered the penthouse, his home. Seen the evidence of another person, this person inhabiting his home.

Her practical canvas sneakers were toed off next to the coat stand.

The hold all, which held her bridal finery was open at a table. She'd folded everything he'd given her into a neat pile and kept it there, on display.

All day, yesterday, he'd had the nagging feeling something was wrong. Awfully, epically wrong.

He shouldn't have done what he'd done. Ensnared this young woman, for she was so young, for his own ends. It felt ruthless on a different level.

Seeing the things he'd bought her, the things she'd married him in, with no protest, no histrionics had sucker punched that feeling of ruthlessness into him.

God, what had he done?

Then, the smell of roasting meat and potatoes had hit him. Homey. *Inviting.* He'd followed it to the kitchen where he'd found her. Head buried in a textbook, bathed in a small pool of light that shouldn't have been fucking *romantic* but was.

And he'd hurtled down to a dark place. A place where the words that came out of him belonged to someone else. Someone who did not have his infinity capacity for control.

And what frightened him, he who had no fear left at all, was the single tempting smile she'd given him when he'd almost barked at her. It was soft and female and homey. *Inviting.*

Come in, that smile said. *Stay. It's safe here.*

But Drake knew nothing was safe. Nothing in this world that wasn't controlled by him. Not the air, not the earth and certainly not a woman who'd declared war on him so brazenly.

So, he'd destroyed her gratitude and gone into this office to steadily work his way through the wine along with one-fifths of a bottle of Jim Beam and a stack of ever-present paperwork. Convinced he'd done the right thing for both of them.

Not even knowing when he'd passed out.

~~~~~
~~~~~

"Drake…Drake, man," Dan whistled shrilly. "Are you even listening to me? You look horror-struck," he said bluntly.

Drake reined his wandering mind back to the conversation. To business. To what was safe. "Sorry, man." He attempted a weak smile. "I'm famished. Can you give me a second while I grab something to eat?"

Dan settled back in his chair, an incredible view of Sydney Harbor highlighted behind him. Australia was two hours ahead, so he was dressed for business. In a sharp brown suit with clean lines and a precisely knotted tie in salmon pink. Drake wouldn't be surprised if the man wore suspenders.

Drake swiftly stacked an empty plate with a cold steak, ladled the sauce liberally over it and scooped two helpings of the potatoes and greens.

He sat down at the table, placing the tab before him, raised his knife and fork to Dan. "You don't mind, do you?"

Dan shook his head. "Go ahead. You look like you need it."

"So, here's what I've been thinking since our last conversation. It's not about the land, is it?" Drake cut the steak into precise bites and speared one with the sauce and a tiny bit of potato, while he spoke.

He popped the bite into his mouth and almost rolled his eyes back in ecstasy. "Jesus, this is amazing."

"I don't understand what you mean, Drake. What's not about the land?" Dan sounded a little concerned.

Drake didn't blame him.

Dan was the co-founder and partner of Hallaran & Houston, a globally famous, award-winning architecture firm. He'd founded it with his college mate, Jordan Hallaran, a genius at structural creativity, while Dan was the operational brains of the outfit.

Drake had done his research thoroughly before deciding to work with Hallaran & Houston for his future project, starting with the Singapore complex. They were progressive, eco-fanatics and almost always delivered under budget. Ergo, perfect for him.

"What I mean, Dan." Drake paused to finish half the steak. "Is that building this complex is as much a symbolic gesture as it is an actual business move. And yes, I know we need to find the space we need ASAP and break ground, like yesterday but…from where I'm standing, I think." He chewed on the potatoes – they were buttery, delicious, melt in your mouth perfect.

"Do you want to be alone with the food, Fallahil?" Dan was openly laughing at him now. "You look almost orgasmic."

I'd like to be alone with the chef. The thought freaked him out.

Drake shot Dan the bird and finished chewing, before answering. "I think, we are thinking too small.

See, if Singapore's who's who won't welcome me and my business with open arms, it's time to take it elsewhere."

"You're moving?"

Drake shook his head, as the idea, floated again. The one that had taken root inside his head yesterday, after Anya had offered him her neck so sweetly, so obediently because she was so fucking grateful to him for giving her what she wanted.

"I'm not moving anywhere. But maybe it's time to scare these fucking entitled pricks into thinking I am. Can I trust you and your company to work with my real estate acquisitions team and submit bids in Nagpur, India, Phnom Penh, Vietnam, Kathmandu, Nepal, Bhutan's capital, Kandy, Sri Lanka --"

"Dude, give me a second to take all of this down." Dan straightened from his slouch, whipped out his Mont Blanc and started jotting the names of the places down.

"Don't forget Jo'burg in South Africa, Kinhasa in Nigeria and Addis Ababa in Ethiopia, and for good measure add Alexandria to the list."

Dan went through the list of names while Drake got himself seconds of everything and methodically demolished the contents of his plate. He felt infinitely better, satiated even, by the time he was done.

The food was fucking divine and so was his idea.

Sure, he'd have to work all this off with a brisk full body workout but it was totally worth it.

In fact, Drake thought smugly, scraping the last of the potatoes off his plate, he'd earned it for being so fucking smart.

Dan looked up. His normally quiescent expression was troubled. "These are all places the Runwals and your new business partners, the Chans, have holdings in."

"Yep." Drake settled with his hands behind his head, the robe gaping open. "They are."

"Are you trying to fuck over the people you're doing business with, Fallahil?" Dan asked quietly.

Drake shook his head. "No," he answered quickly. "I'm absolutely not. I just…" He gave a grin that could only be construed as nasty. "Need to remind everyone who I really am."

Dan nodded, but he didn't look convinced. "And you think strong-arming your way into…" He consulted the sheet again. "Seventeen countries is the way to do it."

Drake shrugged, the picture of supreme arrogance. "What else do I have to do with my time anyway, Dan?"

Dan shook his head. "I don't understand you money men, Drake. I'm so glad I stick to honest-to-god working with my hands over whatever it is you do."

"I'm glad," Drake said cheerfully. He gave a tiny burp as his stomach signaled fulfilment. "You and Jordan are the best outfit in town and I'd hate to take my business away from you."

Dan's lips twitched. "Jordan's going to be a hard sell on this one, Drake. He doesn't like playing games with people's livelihoods."

I'll buy controlling interest in the bank and shut it down.

"Jordan's a better man than I am. Unlike you, Dan," Drake said bluntly. "See, Jordan didn't come from wealth like you, did he? So it doesn't have the same hold on him, like it does on you."

Dan leaned back, wary and tense. All traces of geniality vanished from his expression. "You come from nothing too, Fallahil, have you forgotten?"

Not for a second. Not ever. "I'm aware of who I am, Houston. But the question you have to answer is this – what do you want, Dan? Do you want to be a good man and friend or a better businessman and feed the gods of profit?"

Dan tapped his Mont Blanc. "I'll run the idea past Jordan and come back to you with an action plan."

"It's a pleasure doing business with you, my man."

Drake ended the call before Dan could finish saying 'Fuck you.'

When he was done, he rose from the chair, and washed the utensils he'd used in the little sink on the island.

He felt a strange stirring before he was done. As if the air had thickened, heated into something else.

"I didn't think you knew how to use the dishwashing liquid."

~ ~ ~ ~ ~

Drake carefully placed the plate on the drying rack before turning back.

Anya stood there in yesterday's clothes – the jeans rumpled over her ankles and the tucked in sweatshirt slipping to reveal one golden, rounded shoulder. Her hair was in clumps over a patently furious face.

"Good morning." He spoke carefully.

She gave his own less-than-perfect appearance a scornful look.

He wasn't sure but he thought he detected heat when she saw his bare chest with its light dusting of hair. He wasn't into manscaping and, honestly, didn't have the time for it. And if she liked it, he was all for it!

"Don't you dare be nice to me after last night!"

"I wasn't," he agreed quickly.

"I have some things to say to you," Anya barreled on without having heard him.

She untucked the sweatshirt from her jeans and he glimpsed the curves of her belly.

His mouth watered at the thought of tasting it, as if he'd not eaten a whole heap of food.

"Anya," he began just as quickly.

"No!" The word cut through him with the slickness of a hot knife. "I talk, you listen." She pointed at her chest then his, drawing his attention to it.

He was famished all over again.

Drake prudently covered the front of his boxers with the robe and tied it.

"I agreed to your feudal arrangement because things… people other than me would have been harmed if I hadn't. I know you have no conscience, I've experienced it first-hand, so I can't allow you to do that to someone else."

Drake blinked. Said nothing. Little stings erupting in his skin at her pointed words.

"But, if you think that I am going to let you treat me like…like…I am your *staff* then you're mistaken, Mr. Fallahil. Epically." She practically threw the words at him. Her tawny eyes shooting flames.

"I was trying to do something nice for you yesterday. A mistake I won't repeat ever again. But I will not allow you to talk to me or treat me that way. Ever again. Are we clear?"

"Crystal," he said somberly.

"We're married." Her lips quivered at the words but she plowed on. "And I expect to be treated with a modicum of dignity and respect. Can you manage that?"

Drake nodded. Rubbed a hand on his face and waved his hand at the food. For some reason, words tumbled out of his mouth. "No one's ever cooked for me apart from my…family."

"What?" Now it was her turn to blink. "What was that?"

Desire rose swift and unpredictable inside him, heating up his blood and nearly turning his brain off. He almost allowed it. Almost. It was easier to control the desire than his need to tell her the truth.

"I said." He took a couple of steps so they were closer than they'd been, with the length of the table between them. "No one has ever cooked for me before. The women…my partners…preferred dining out or a personal chef."

Anya smiled bitterly. "What a privileged life they must lead."

"They have. But, I know them. I know their attitudes. The workings of their brain," Drake said slowly.

He couldn't stop looking at her. Couldn't take his eyes off her elfin face. She didn't even realize how close he was till he almost towered over her. He wanted her outrageously because even when she did, she just raised her chin higher and glared at him. Disdain clear in the slim lines of her body.

"I understand what they want and how they react when they get what they want." His murmur was almost to himself, as if he was just now seeing her for what she truly was.

Different from every other woman he'd ever met.

"Yeah, they're fucking empty dolls," she muttered.

"You're not." The words dropped between them.

Anya swallowed her angry words down.

He knew it because he kept looking at her eyes. They were blazing with righteous fury. And he wanted them… wanted *her* compliant and hazy.

He wanted her. Period. Under him, while he took her to the edge and lost himself inside her, found the one thing he'd always searched for in every woman he'd been with. Absolution.

"You're real. And human. And…" He searched for the right word. He himself rigid with the effort to not touch her. Because he'd done enough damage to her.

"And what?" He really hoped her voice was that soft and breathy. Not just a product of his own desire.

"Fair," he finished, at last. "You're fair, Anya."

She touched her cheek. Where part of her hair was smashed against the soft skin. Brushed it impatiently back. "I'm not fair. I don't believe in justice over revenge."

"That's not the fair I meant."

"Then what do you…"

Anya took a step back because she finally, *finally* realized how close they were. Their toes and torsos almost touching each other.

Her expressive eyes dropped, unbidden, to the parted robe and he knew she was interested. More than interested. Because her lips parted, her nostrils flared, and dark color stained her cheeks.

It would be so easy, so very easy to just reach for her right now and do what he really wanted.

Devour her.

He had a very explicit image of doing exactly that.

Whipping that swaddling sweatshirt off her, while he nipped and sucked at her generous breasts. While he unzipped her jeans and plunged into her hot, wet depths. Right where they stood. All control gone, left to the winds.

He knew she'd let him, because bodies didn't lie. And hers was telegraphing need clearly. It would be glorious, make him feel better than all the food had.

"Mr. Fallahil," she whispered. She was staring at his eyes. Hypnotized by them. Aware of the need licking his veins and turning his own blood against him.

Drake bent down, just an inch. "Call me Drake, Anya," he ordered.

He spoke near her ear, barely touching her. But his breath stirred her hair and he smelled soft, warm, fragrant woman.

"Dr…Drake, what are you doing?"

His name, spoken in her tremulous voice acted as a return to logic. What was he doing?!

He straightened up. "Cleaning up after an excellent meal," he replied conversationally. "What else would I be doing?"

Anya's eyes dropped to his chest again. He willed his heart to beat at its normal pace. The tip of her tongue peeked out before it darted inside again.

Fuck. He needed to get away from her before he forgot her rules of consent. And did something that would only prove her right.

"Nothing," she murmured. "Absolutely nothing." She looked at the table, the demolished mountain of food. "You enjoyed it?"

Drake nodded rapidly. "I loved it." He even gave her a semi-authentic smile. "Thank you for your kindness, Anya. I appreciate it even though I don't deserve it."

She made a restless movement with her shoulders. "It's okay. I mean…."

"I know what you mean." He stood aside to let her past him. "Did you wake up to see your mom off before she goes for surgery?"

"Yes. I didn't want to miss seeing her, before she…she was taken in." Anya nodded. Looking for all the world like a lost little girl.

He couldn't help himself then.

He touched her shoulder.

She let him.

"Can I…May I give you a hug?"

She gave him a wordless glance. But stepped closer and immediately, forcefully put her arms around him. Burying her head in his chest. Her breath shuddered out, a long, painful exhale.

He held her for a long, comforting moment, cupping her skull, learning the shape and texture of her hair.

He said nothing. Because worry for her parent was palpable in her. And there was nothing he could say that would take it away.

"The car's coming for you in twenty. Will you be ready by then?"

Anya nodded. "Yeah. I'll be ready."

"Okay, then." He made to step back but her arms tightened fractionally against him. He felt ten feet tall at that.

Anya ended the hug. Gave him another tremulous glance, her eyes were golden warm again. The strident look gone. "It's nice to know you keep your word, Drake."

"A deal's a deal," he agreed, while feelings…alien and uncomfortable burst into life inside him. And he couldn't make sense of them. They just *were*.

"And you always honor your deal, don't you?"

"Always."

"I'll remember that the next time you're beastly to me." Her full lips twitched and he allowed her to get away with the parting shot.

After all, he figured, he deserved much more than that. And she was just the woman to let him have it.

EIGHTEEN

"Don't fuss over me, Anu," Swati murmured as Anya fussed with her hypoallergenic pillow for the nth time. "I'm *fine.*"

Swati sounded so much stronger than she had been four days ago, when she'd come out of surgery, a little groggy and a lot in pain. But, her bow-shaped legs were arrow straight and in padded straps following the surgery.

"You're more than fine, Mama. You're amazing." Anya kissed her mom's cheek and felt a rush of gratitude and awe at her strength.

Swati swung her legs off her bed and beckoned Anya to sit next to her. Anya sat and hugged her mom sideways. Swati tapped on the bracelet gracing Anya's wrist. It spelled *Anika* in hammered aluminum, of all metals.

"Anika?" She quirked her brows.

Anya smiled weakly. "It's a private joke, mama. Drake's got a weird sense of humor." It was also eco-conscious, since aluminum was the most durable and recyclable of all metals.

"I bet." Swati smiled. Then it faded into something soft, concerned. "You don't have to be here all the time, Anya. I am doing so much better now than I did last week."

Anya cried copiously when she'd seen her mother take her first tentative steps with the walker at the physical therapist's recommendation just a few hours after surgery. And, every day since then, her mom improved bit by bit. Sometimes complaining, sometimes sweating but always moving.

It was a fucking miracle.

And the man who'd made it all possible was, impossibly, the man she was married to.

"Of course, I'm going to be here, Mama. School's out for summer, thank god. So I don't have classes to attend anymore. Where else would I be?" Anya asked with a little laugh.

Swati gave her a pointed glance. "At home? With Drake? Taking care of him. I know he works way too hard for a man of his age."

Thirty-eight, Anya thought with inner shock. Drake was almost fourteen years older than her. Yet, he kept going with the energy of a man in his twenties. On some kind of an upper. Except, the strongest drug she'd seen him take was those caffeinated drinks he preferred.

The more she came to know of Drake, the more she was beginning to respect him.

He slept four hours a night, could rattle the P&L statements of all of his various concerns – and they numbered in the hundreds – and remembered the names of all his employees.

That made the least sense of all. Why would a man in his position with his kind of power care about the people in his life, ensuring it ran with the smoothness of an electric hybrid?

The conclusion she kept coming back to was – he wasn't the beast he wanted everyone to think he was.

Anya kept her face neutral when she answered her mother. "Drake doesn't need me to take care of him, mama. He has a plethora of staff to do that."

"But you're his bride. Don't you want to spend time with him?" Swati asked curiously.

Anya kept her sigh to herself. She swung down from the bed. "I spend plenty of time with him, mama. Trust me, it's all fine. In fact." She smiled happily. "Drake even suggested bringing you home with us to the penthouse for your recuperation."

"Oh no! No, Anya." Swati shook her head vehemently. "I'm not going to come and impose in your new life with your new husband."

"But, mama, the rehab has to continue for at least six weeks more. You need help getting around. And our home is not exactly crutch-friendly," Anya argued logically.

Their dinky three-bedsit in Little India had tiny doorways and narrow passages which made maneuvering difficult on the best of days. Plus, the bathroom and toilet were almost on top of each other.

"I'll manage. I always have, haven't I?"

"You'll be alone," Anya nearly wailed the word out. She'd been counting on having her mom home with her, in the huge cavernous penthouse with the supertree almost poking in. "I have already made all the arrangements…"

"Then unmake them," Swati cut in, firmly. "I'm not crashing your honeymoon with your husband. We have foregone every single tradition with your hasty wedding. I said nothing because you deserve to be happy and in love. But, this I'm not doing, Anya. I'm not going to be a monster-in-law."

Anya stared in dismay at her mother. "Drake is happy to have you…"

"He's a newly married man. He does not want his mother-in-law taking up space in his life."

Anya shook her head. "Mama, it's not like that."

"I'm your mother, Anya. What I say, goes." Swati said in a tone of utter finality. And she looked pugnacious enough to carry her words out, considering she was still a patient.

~~~~~~

Anya reflected on her mother's words as she took the MRT back to Marina Bay station, after sharing a catered,
~~~~~~

nutritious lunch with her mom. She did not want to go back to the modern museum Drake called home.

The place echoed with rarified air and a silence bordering on oppressive.

She'd shamelessly snooped through the whole fifty thousand square foot apartment and discovered the *bathroom* with its own Olympic size swimming pool and the tree poking in. She'd seen the master suite and found it depressingly devoid of any personal effects. The office was messy and cluttered, with a filing system that probably only made sense to Drake.

Anya'd gone through some of the files and was boggled by the sums and terms in the contracts.

He had a finger in practically every industry invented on God's earth. And he kept track of them all, on a regular basis.

She'd kept herself out of his office after that. And focused on taking care of her mother.

Thankfully, her phone buzzed before she was dragged down by more despondent thoughts.

Anya answered it with pathetic eagerness. "Hey, Mili. How are you?"

"I'm great, Anya," Mili's dulcet voice floated through the phone. She sounded vastly different on the phone – someone warm and *sexy* when Anya knew for a fact she was a proper corporate barracuda. "How are you?"

"I'm…bored," Anya confessed. She gave a nervous chuckle, pushed a hand through her hair. Realized it needed a wash. "Forget I said that, will you?"

"Forgotten," Mili replied prompty. "But, if I may ask, why are you not feeling bored?"

Anya looked out the window of the speeding train. It only took forty minutes to reach from one end of the city to the other. One of the things she loved most about Singapore. But, today, she wished the journey would take longer.

"My mom says she doesn't want to come home with me for her recuperation. She wants to be independent," Anya said softly.

"That's a good thing, isn't it? Swati Aunty is learning to stand on her own two feet, pun totally intended."

"Yes, but." Anya sighed.

"But you're feeling sad because she doesn't need you anymore, aren't you?" Mili pinpointed the heart of Anya's issue accurately.

"Yeah," Anya admitted. "With school being out and Mom shooing me away, I have nothing to do and I…am not used to it. Does that make me uncool?"

"Of course not, babe. Enjoy yourself," Mili advised. "Take the summer off. Sunbathe in that ridiculously beautiful bathroom?"

"That bathroom freaks me out," Anya confessed. "It has a tree poking in!"

Mili laughed. "You're the only person in the world I know who's freaked out by the trappings of wealth."

"But I'm not wealthy, Mili," Anya protested. "None of this is mine. Did you know that the first three floors of the Trident has staff quarters so I don't even have to clean the penthouse? I can't fathom living like that."

Mili had nothing to say to that. "Drake's super-efficient, you know. He'd not want someone like you with your brain using your time vacuuming the house."

"He's super-efficient and self-sufficient," Anya said slowly.

And he damn well did not need her too.

Drake made his own coffee when he woke up for meetings at ungodly hours, cleaned up after himself, all while working on whatever corporate maneuver occupied his immediate attention. He wasn't picky about food or anything, really. In fact, the vainest thing about him were the cut and quality of his clothes, perfectly coordinated and tailored to perfection.

It was unfortunate he had the physique to look divine in them all.

"Is he always like this?" Anya asked while her heart thudded loudly.

"Like what?"

"*On* all the time. Like his brain never stops working."

Mili laughed, a rich amused sound. "Yes. That's accurate. Drake's the most focused individual it's been my privilege to know. He never stops. It's kind of hot, isn't it?"

It *was.*

Because, to her secret shame, she'd wondered too often, what would it be like to have him bestow all that focus on her… while she was in his arms. Naked. Or at least, half-naked.

She'd thought, far too often, of his sculpted chest revealed so tantalizingly through the silk robe, black silk boxers hugging muscled thighs tapering to well-shaped calves. The one and only time she'd caught him like that.

She'd been so *angry,* heartbroken at the callous way he'd treated her on what was supposed to be their wedding day. But, one look at him in the robe and she'd almost lost her ability to reason.

Then, he'd turned the tables on her and been *reasonable* with her. Even platonically hugged her. His big hand cupping her head to his steady beating chest till all the chaos calmed down in her and she'd breathed easy in hours.

She dreamed of that hug far too often for it to be normal.

How well they fit together, like two puzzle pieces – one big and another petite – and still somehow worked. How her rounded edges melted into his hardness and found home there. He'd actually come through for her another time she needed him to.

And she…Anya sighed.

"That's too mournful a sigh for you, Anya. So I'm going to rescue you," Mili said decisively. "You know what? Why don't you come into the office? I'm sure I can find some project for you to tackle."

Anya's eyes brightened. "You'd do that for me? Will Drake mind?"

"Fuck him," Mili said cheerfully. "If he is too stupid to leave his quasi-new and brilliant bride alone then he deserves to pay for it. How soon can you get here?"

Anya looked at her outfit for the day. It was a simple cotton tee shirt with the picture of a unicorn shooting rainbows and a mini-skirt in deference to the warm weather. Her shoes were lace up espadrilles because it was summer, after all.

She carried a light jacket in case the night air turned chilly, but so far, it hadn't.

"That depends on if you think unicorn tees are business casual?"

Mili gave a laugh that sounded like a witch's cackle. Slightly evil and very naughty. "We at Fallahil Inc do not give a shit if you prance around in fig leaves as long as you're on-task."

"On task, I can be, ma'am."

"Awesome. I'll see you in thirty minutes, then?"

~ ~ ~ ~ ~

And so, three hours later, Anya found herself carting files and documents, fetched coffee for the other team members in the office, and became friends with the hardest taskmaster of all – Mili Iyer.

She'd been given a table and an office laptop in Mili's office, a floor below Drake's, apparently. And so she didn't even have to be around Drake, which was just fine.

At around eleven pm, Mili fluffed her hair out of the stylish Burberry trench she wore over her uber-feminine powder green dress flirting at her knees. "Are you sure, you want to continue, Anya?"

Anya was busy listing salient points on a company acquisition deal in Sri Lanka from last year, so Drake could figure out the systems process behind it and replicate it in Bangladesh.

"Hmmm? Yeah," she murmured distractedly.

Mili left with a goodnight Anya barely heard. She was fascinated by the details of this deal, as she'd been by all the specifics she'd seen today.

Drake was, without doubt, the man who'd write the future the way he saw fit. With his knowledge of changing global economies, his almost uncanny sense of manipulating a stock market right before the position changed, the man had never not tasted success. He'd done so by never cutting corners – with any kind of resource.

It was, frankly, awe-inspiring.

Anya finished typing the end on the document, when the door to Mili's cabin blasted open and the object of her inspiration stormed in.

"What are you--?" Drake frowned. Looked around. "Where's Mili?"

"Mili's done for the day. I was almost done too." Anya stood up and shut the laptop. "Did you need something?"

"Yes, I…The Tahana file. Mili was supposed to email it to me before she left." His eyes bored into her skull. "What are you *doing* here?"

"I work here." She powered open the laptop, a prototype predicted to take over the market when it launched next year. "I mean, I'm interning here because obviously I'm not being paid for my labor." She laughed lightly to take the sting off her barb. "Is Tahana spelled with one 'A' or two?"

"One 'A', both times," Drake said shortly. "What do you mean you're interning here?"

Anya, pulled the relevant file from the system. "I'll email this to you in a second. Mili offered me a position here when I told her I'm free for the summer."

She gave him a tentative smile. "I didn't think you'd mind. You don't, do you?"

He narrowed his eyes, and one muscle ticked in his sculpted jaw.

Anya logged the stubble that had sprouted in the last few hours on his cheeks. Had the bizarre urge to press her lips to it. Feel the rough texture against her soft skin.

She immediately dismissed it as an impossible thought.

"I'd like to see you in my office when you're done, Anya. Can you do that?"

Anya nodded. "Sure thing." She gave him a three-fingered salute and a cheeky wink. "Sir."

NINETEEN

For the first time ever, Drake could not focus on the document in front of him. The numbers on the screen might as well be in Klingon. All he could see was Anya, *his wife,* bent over the computer, his office computer, looking years younger than her actual age – twenty four. Her cheeks were flushed with energy and there was a light in her eyes he'd *never* seen.

Not since he'd become acquainted with her. Lived with her. And that was a special hell he could not unpack yet.

Her energy was palpable as she'd smiled and winked at him.

Called him *sir.*

As if it was an inside joke, one he should heartily laugh about. As if he'd employ someone who looked and talked and smelled like her.

She ripped through his concentration even without trying.

It enraged him.

Obviously, he was going to have to fire her.

Drake realized he was gripping the stylus too tightly, and eased his grip on the device. His focus came rushing back and he continued cross-checking the numbers on The Bloomberg – a series of high-function monitors producing large reams of numbers simultaneously on different screens.

He was almost done when there was a timid knock on the door before it opened with a small swoosh. He cataloged her entry into the office, the progress of her light footfalls as she came to a stop at the desk.

The absurd keychain hanging on her backup entered the periphery of his vision. *Was that a superhero figure?!*

"I'm here," Anya said lightly. "As requested, sir."

Drake finished looking at the last row of numbers he needed to before approving the documents. They swished off before he lifted his head and appraised her.

~ ~ ~ ~ ~

Today, her hair was pinned back in a single fat braid that hung artfully over her shoulder. She wore a cream-color jacket over a tee shirt with unicorns on it. Her skirt was at least two inches higher than was office-regulation.

Wasn't it?

Anya snapped her fingers. Continued smiling at him, artlessly. "Can I just say this? I can't imagine keeping track of everything you own and do and are, Drake. I mean, it's mammoth on a scale I can't even describe. And

Mili's just so perfect at everything, isn't she? I've learned so much from her already."

"Who said you could work here, Anya?" Drake asked quietly.

She perched on the edge of his desk. Her petite legs dangling over the side, the skirt riding another inch over her slim thigh, revealing more of her golden skin.

His vision hazed until he clutched the stylus again.

She turned around, and gave him an earnest look. "Mili did, Drake. She's a little swamped since one of her team's off on maternity. And I am totally free and available since school's out for the summer. So--"

"So, you two decided you could take up a position in the company?"

Anya nodded and the braid moved with her. Bringing attention to her breasts jutting out of the fucking unicorn tee shirt. "Yeah. It's the best work ex I could get, to be honest. Learning from the best. Besides, you have nothing to worry about."

He cocked his head up. Speared her with a cool glance. "I don't?"

"Yep. Since I'm only a glorified gopher, you don't have to pay me anything. So we're not technically violating the terms of your pre-nup. And I..."

"Fuck the pre-nup. I don't want you here, Anya," he said bluntly.

She opened her unpainted mouth once, then shut it. All the animation leached out of her. Bit by bit. Her tawny eyes were opaque when she asked, "May I ask why you don't want me here?"

"Because." He leaned forward in his chair so she could see the derision and power clearly in him. "You're not my intern, unpaid or not."

"Then what am I?"

"You're my…" The word stuck in his throat. He cleared it. "You're under my employ. But this is not in your job description."

"Then what is?" She challenged.

Anya hopped off from the table and rounded the expanse so she stood over him. A tiny avenging angel in a unicorn tee shirt and spotless white sneakers. Her mobile face blazed with righteous anger.

She shook her hand at him. "Is it in my job description to wear meaningless pieces of jewelry?" She almost ripped the bracelet which had Anika linked in lightweight platinum. "Like this?" Threw it at him, so he had to catch it.

Drake shrugged, feeling more in control now that she was losing it. "It was a gag gift. Since Anika Jalan's birthday was yesterday. I thought you'd appreciate the whimsy."

Her jaw worked furiously. "Whimsy?" She repeated.

Then she tapped the other piece of jewelry she wore. The enormous sapphire, which hugged the valley of her breasts so perfectly, drawing his gaze there. "This wasn't whimsical, was it? This was a consolation prize for my… what was it you said, acquiescence? You know what, Mr. Fallahil, truce is over." She took the necklace and placed it on the table.

"You can't buy my acquiescence. Any more than you can assign a value to my time and effort."

He raised his hands. "Why not?"

"Because I'm a person. And I have feelings and opinions and you're not my boss. Mili hired me. She can fire me if she wants to."

"I could fire Mili. Then she won't be around to hire you or fire you, will she?" He asked silkily.

Anya's eyes flashed a second before he realized her intent. She reached out and gave him a roundhouse to the jaw. The sound reverberated with her accelerated breathing.

His head snapped back, absorbing the impact of the blow.

She took an immediate step back. Her eyes filled slowly with horror at what she'd done.

Drake stood up. Slowly. Resisting the urge to touch his tender jaw. Her punch was surprisingly effective.

Anya stared at her closed fist, with the thumb tucked in. then at his jaw, which was a lot closer than it had been a moment ago.

Drake smiled, gleaming. "Do you think I won't hit you back just because you're a woman?"

His jaw ached a little with each word he spoke but adrenalin displaced the pain. Turned it into a slick heat coursing through his body.

She took a trembling breath as she stumbled back once more. "I…I'm sorry. I'm so sorry, I hit you. That wasn't well-done of me."

"No," he agreed gravely. "It really wasn't." He took another step toward her, aware of time itself slowing down so each movement echoed and amplified.

The regret in her lovely eyes. The fatness of her braid. The slim line of her. The agitated rise and fall of her chest.

Anya shook her head. "You know what?" She spoke in a hurry. "You're right. I don't know what I was thinking. Working here is a bad idea. A very bad idea."

"Yes," he agreed. "It really is."

With a single sweep of his arms he gathered her close and placed her on the glass desk before she could make another sound.

~~~~~

Her eyes rounded, in sheer terror and bewilderment. The tip of her pink tongue peeked out between her pursed lips.
~~~~~

"What are you doing?" Anya whispered.

Drake leaned down, down so their eyes were level. So she could see him for what he truly was. A man undone, his control hanging by the last tether.

She leaned away from him instinctively, placing her palms on either side of her.

"What do you want me to do, Anya?" The slick heat inside of him turned taut, ready to lean into violence or rampant lust. He would welcome either.

But he'd given her his word. And he would keep it. He'd not touch her without consent.

"Drake…" His name was a bottomless whisper from her lips.

"What do you want, Anya?" The words were just short of a guttural growl. "Do you want me to retaliate for hitting me?"

She looked mesmerized, her breath suspended between her chest and her mouth.

He was aware that his own breath was a shorter than it had been. Because the image of doing exactly that, using his palm on her skin – to arouse and soothe – rose in him.

His blood ran thick, thicker, pooling well south of his brain until his arousal hurt him.

Drake bent over her, still not touching her. Still keeping his distance.

Anya automatically opened her legs so he could step between them.

"Or?" She whispered.

"Or," he parroted after her. "I could retaliate in a different way. The choice is yours."

"And if I say no to either?" Her voice was so breathy, her lashes almost drifted shut. He could see her nipples peaking under the thin material of her tee shirt.

He smiled. Slow and predatory. Certain of his victory. He leaned close, closer than he had, placed his own palms a scant centimeter away from hers on either side so he caged her in place without touching any part of her.

The air swam with unrestrained desire. His. Hers. He could hardly tell anymore.

"Why would you want to, Anya?" He spoke near her ear, his breath stirring her hair.

She turned her head a scant inch and there her lips were. Parted and ripe. His for the taking.

His wife looked at him for a second that stretched into eternity.

"I don't."

~ ~ ~ ~ ~

Anya reared into him and crashed her mouth against his. Her hands spearing into his hair, gripping his skull as she kissed him like a woman starving.

His heart slowed down for a beat. Then it crash-started into life. Beating so loud and fast it was all he could hear. He clutched at her wrists, and grabbed them. Brought her closer to him.

She moaned, she actually moaned into his mouth.

It jacked his blood up.

He angled his head to the left and she chased it. Diving deep into him, so it felt like he was being ravished by her. The thought was drugging, addictive.

Drake left her wrists and clutched her slim waist. Tugging the tee shirt out of the skirt's waist band.

She sucked on his tongue, and his head swam. He shot his hands up inside her tee shirt, too impatient to wait anymore. Her back was warm, soft…it melted into his touch when he ran his fingers over her spine.

Clutched at her nape so he could kiss her the way he wanted her to. Drawing everything out from her mouth. His other hand closed over her breast and Anya cried out. He did it again, squeezing it against his hard palm.

She arched into him, giving him more access.

He still kissed her, voraciously, needily, as he jerked the neckline of the tee shirt down and cupped her fully.

She was trapped in her own clothing when she tried to get to his waistcoat to open.

Drake changed the angle of the kiss, arching her further over his desk, stepping between the notch of her thighs, her skirt riding so high he could glimpse her inner thighs. It aroused him even further.

Anya finally won the war against his waistcoat, the buttons pinging against the desk. Her touch was hot, frantic…enticing, against him.

She attacked his shirt open, while he continued kissing her, unwilling to give up the miraculous honey of her lips. The softness of her mouth. The sharp scrape of her teeth. The sinuous glide of her tongue.

Anya ran a hand over his abs, and cried out when he squeezed her too hard. Her flesh so warm and willing in his hands he never wanted to let go.

"Sorry," he muttered.

She shook her head and raked a nail down the center of his happy trail. "Don't be."

He jerked her skirt the rest of the way up and she made a choked kind of sound. Squeezing hard on his tongue, as if she could already feel him inside her.

Drake dragged her forward, while she tackled his belt. It swooshed down when she tugged it off, before she dealt with the placket of his flat-front pants and he stirred in his boxers. Hard.

He bent down, breaking the kiss and took her breast in his hot, avid mouth. Drawing a line of open-mouthed kisses from her neck to the top of her breast.

Anya bent back, as if the pressure of his mouth on her was too much for her spine to bear. She clutched at his head, as more sounds emerged from her. Needy, open, *wanting.*

The sounds of their combined breath was heady, hedonistic to him.

Drake tugged the tee shirt further down so it framed her breasts and he licked his lips as he saw the way one brown tip gleamed. He took it in again and swirled the tip in his mouth, feeling it harden and unfurl as he played with it.

Anya wrapped her legs around his hip, undulated against him.

She was wrecked, gone. Her hair curling out from the braid so it formed a halo around her flushed cheeks and red-stained shoulders.

It was the headiest of all things to see.

He swept her off the desk, his hands cupping her hot butt as he dropped in his chair. He squeezed the cheeks rhythmically as he sucked on one breast and then the other and she moved against him.

Anya pushed his shirt off his chest and kissed his shoulders, the corded side of his neck, the sides of his ears, nipping his earlobe when he did something that took her to the edge.

He grew more when she sucked on his earlobe, and she gave a breathless little laugh at that.

In retaliation, Drake ripped her bikini panties at the side hem and plunged one long, hot finger into her.

~ ~ ~ ~ ~

Anya cried out as she clutched the back of the chair at the sheer sensation of having him inside her. Her head thrown back.

He gritted his teeth and fought to keep his control. He combed through her braid so her hair fell in waves around her back, entwining some of it in his fist.

He wanted to hold it in his hand, tugging it while she knelt at his feet and loved him with her mouth.

Drake inserted another finger, crooking his thumb over her clitoris and she cascaded around him. Coating his fingers.

"Please," she gasped.

"Please, what?" He spoke around her tender flesh.

Taking more in his mouth, feeling her everywhere around him. Wet, warm female who was about to explode in his arms. The. Best. Thing. Ever.

"Please, please don't stop."

He shook his head. "Not possible. Open up for me, baby."

Anya moved her legs farther apart, settling against his hard thighs more fully. He reared up a little, so he could kiss her. Wet and wild and deep, shoving his tongue down her throat like he wanted to his cock.

She clutched his back. Ran restless, desperate hands over his spine to find some purchase, some release from the tumult he was creating in her. So effortlessly.

Drake's skin was on fire everywhere she touched him. Till she came to the thick ridged scars right on his shoulder blades. One on each side, as if he'd been given angel wings.

She pressed into them, her touch questing and gentle. Unnerving him.

He shook her off with a heave of his shoulders.

"Hold on," he instructed as he somehow managed to delve his other hand between them and shuck his boxers and pants down.

Anya opened dazed, glassy eyes. Her eyes were enormous, her lips plump and a little bruised from his kisses and the razor burn. She'd never looked more desirable as she did right then.

"Drake." She ran a shaking hand over his hair, cupping his skull before moving down to his nape. "Drake," she said again. Her warmth was scant inches away and he needed in like he needed to fucking breathe.

"I'm clean," Drake gritted out. "Are you on birth control?"

She shook her head. "No."

He closed his eyes, almost in pain from the effort of not pounding into her. With effort, he reached into the back of his trousers and extracted a condom packet.

She tore it with sharp, tiny teeth and he wore it, while kissing her over and over and over. She cupped his jaw in both hands, holding him immobile with the gentle benediction of her kiss.

Finally, he was sheathed and he…

TWENTY

Drake groaned, out loud, as he slid her onto his hard, aching length. She gasped, a soundless movement of her lips as she held his neck.

"Take me," she whispered in his ears. Descending over his length with a trembling breath.

He hoisted her up so, she rose above him, and closed his teeth over one stiff nipple, sucking on it while he pumped into her, a slow glide. Anya moved her hips against him. He did it once, twice, thrice, five times, until he felt her inner muscles clenching against him.

Then he rubbed at her clitoris and she gasped again, fastening her teeth against his neck.

He fisted her hair in his hand, and tugged her head up. His hips moved quicker, of their own violation, his flesh needing something his brain couldn't possibly provide anymore.

Anya started to come, her lips parted in a soundless O.

They stared at each other, breaths suspended.

Tangled in each other as he took her over the edge. Before following himself in a breathless, agonized rush that surprised the fuck out of him.

Drake kissed her with all the intensity of his orgasm, as if he could physically contain it within him and her.

His lips bruising in their punishment, while colors, sounds, the very universe exploded behind his tightly shut lids.

~ ~ ~ ~ ~

When he came to, Drake was slumped at her neck, his legs trembling while she made lazy, little sounds that sounded like music to his ears. She ran timid fingers up and down his biceps, poking little half-moons into his skin.

He loved it.

"You…" He breathed.

Drake blinked, trying to get his breath, oxygen, his fucking brain back.

"You." Anya smiled softly.

She moved to his back. Touched the scar on his right shoulder blade softly.

Drake couldn't help it. He shuddered for a long, tense moment.

"Does it still hurt?"

He shook his head, brushed a soft kiss against the fragrant side of her neck. Right where a pulse beat thick and strong against her skin. "No. Nothing hurts now."

To his actual surprise, he actually meant it.

Anya bit her lip and looked at him for another wordless moment. A thousand emotions and questions came and went in her eyes.

She was flushed, breathless, *lovely* in a way he couldn't quite comprehend as she slumped into him. Her bare chest grazing his, still joined to him after what could only be described as the most intense sexual encounter of her life.

He cocked his head to the side. His waves were all disheveled after the way she'd gripped him. So tight and needy. "Like what you see?"

~~~~~~

Anya couldn't say a word to save her life. She felt, unmoored. Apart from herself.

Not sure, exactly of the mental steps that had led to her half-naked in his arms. Replete from the most amazing orgasm she'd experienced in… forever.

He smiled, the lines bracketing his brilliant eyes – now dimmed by contentment and afterglow – somehow deeper. As if they'd etched into his skin from the force of the pleasure they'd brought each other.

"Anya?"

She opened her mouth, sure the words would come to her when there was a knock on the door. And then, to her utter shock and dismay, the massive doors actually slid open and the most stunning woman stepped in.

~~~~~~

Anya had an impression of tall, statuesque, perfect beauty in a severe pantsuit and sharp red heels, miles of black hair before he ducked her head into his sweaty chest.

The contentment filming her…Drake's face, limning his eyes, faded into stardust.

He was back to his cool impenetrable self as he swiftly swung the chair away so she was mostly hidden from sight.

"Who the fuck let you in?" he bit off.

The woman chuckled. A rich and ripe sound. Full of sexual promise. At least, it sounded like that to Anya's hypersensitive ears.

"I didn't know you were…entertaining, Fallahil. I'd not have knocked."

"Aster," Drake said impatiently.

Anya squirmed against him. Wanting to get a good look at this Aster person who showed such familiarity with the man who was still semi-hard *inside* her.

Drake ran one warning hand into her hair, while he twisted his head to the side. "What do you want?"

"To concede defeat gracefully, of course," Aster said sweetly. "My father told me about your recent nuptials and well…a deal's a deal, as you're so fond of saying. So, here you go."

"What?" Drake sounded surprised and a little wary. "What is that?"

"The check for ten million dollars, of course. What else would it be, Drake?" Aster chuckled.

Anya's blood ran cold. At the casual way the woman tossed the humongous sum from her lips. Who was she to have that kind of money lying around to write for a check?

What the hell was going on?

"By the way, does your new bride know you're having some…" She tsked between her teeth. "Office fun while she waits for you at home."

Anya waited, heart thudding, breath held for Drake to set this woman straight. To call her his wife. For *something*.

"Or is she even at home? I mean." Something swished. "We all know how much you like your own space. She's not even staying with you, is she?"

Whoever this Aster woman was, she knew Drake. Her tone was one of easy familiarity. As if she *knew* Drake. Intimately.

Anya's ears went fiery hot as she connected the dots Aster so helpfully laid out for her.

"You need to leave, Aster." Drake spoke evenly.

He was totally calm and in control. His heart was slow and even, strong, certainly. It did not jackrabbit like hers was.

Anya bet that Drake's expression would be of black hole-like calm if she peeked up at him now. She didn't want to, as a small, hopeful part of her heart broke at his words.

"You need to leave the fuck now."

"Don't worry, Drake," Aster's prep school accent was faultless. Imperious. "I'm leaving. I'd wish you a happy marriage."

Drake's built chest moved as he sucked in a breath. His lips grazed the top of Anya's head. And she violently butted against his chin.

"But I wouldn't mean it so I'm just going to say fuck you."

~~~~~~

The doors barely banged shut before Anya scrambled away from Drake, standing on shaking legs. She hastily tugged her shirt up and her skirt down and. Feeling the torn fabric of her panties sliding down her hips.

She couldn't look at him, as she bundled her hair with both shaking hands, giving it a vicious yank and bunning it up at the top of her head.

Anya felt the stretch of her jacket seams as she did so. And, with a sharp pang that echoed in every single part of her newly satiated body, she realized she'd just made love with her jacket on.

Her head swam. Her eyes stung hotly.
~~~~~~

Drake touched her arm.

Anya recoiled from his touch. Her blood ran cold, icing inside her flushed, fulfilled skin. Turning every single bit of pleasure she'd just experienced inside out. Until it felt like she was an endless glacier. Sharp and stony.

Alone.

"Don't touch me."

"Anya, listen…"

She spied a white paper on the desk. Right at the steamy spot where she'd sat, not minutes ago, allowing this man…this *beast* to do what he willed with her.

Anya dove to get the paper but Drake beat her to it. Her eyes flashed with unholy fury but she was forced to look up at him.

He was still the same. A colossus in his prime.

Sure, his golden hair was slightly messed up and his lips were swollen from the force of her kisses. And, he'd somehow managed to discard the condom and zip into his pants in the seconds it had taken her to straighten up.

So there he was in nothing but his pants. His striated chest in full display, athlete's shoulders gleaming with healthy sweat cooling in the perfectly-controlled temperature. The rest of him a tall, golden length that had driven her over the edge of ecstasy.

His eyes burned like beacons on his ruggedly, unfairly handsome face. And she wanted to scratch them out. Wanted to hurt him the way he'd just managed to hurt her.

Killing some essential part of her.

In a kind of distant haze, she saw the precise shape of her teeth marks on his skin. Right where his shoulders bulged into his back. They rippled now when he brought his hand up and handed her the check himself.

Anya took it, taking care to not touch his fingers.

The numbers were right there. Ten million dollars.

She raised dead eyes to him. "Is that USD or Singapore?"

Drake closed his scary eyes. "I'm so sorry, sweetheart."

She threw the check at him. It landed on his chest, slid down. It was an exact replay of the other time they'd done this. When he'd trapped her into this horrid arrangement by threatening to bring chaos and destruction on innocent people.

How could she have forgotten what he really was?

"I hope I'm worth it, Drake. I hope that fuck was worth the money." The ice twisted sharper inside her. Stabbing her.

His lush lips twisted in a grimace. "Anya, please, let me explain."

"She's the ex, isn't she?" she asked distantly. "The one you needed protection from?"

He nodded. "Yes, Aster Chan."

Anya nodded. Felt the movement in her neck, her skull. Which he'd gripped like a lifeline when he'd kissed her past her own breath. "Then my job is done? I never have to see you again."

Drake's hands clenched and she watched it with aloof interest. Then, they loosened, finger by finger. And she had to admire his wretched control. He still did not care. Not really.

"If you could just let me explain." He took one step toward her.

"Where's the bathroom?" she cut in politely.

Receding into a world of practicalities and next steps. Because she had to get out of this room, this space that smelled of their combined musk, when she was still sticky from him and her own desire. Where every breath was a knife wound inside her and she bled infernally.

"It's through there." He pointed at one section of the wall behind him.

She stared unseeingly at it. "I'm going in. I'd like you to not be here when I come back. Will you do that?"

Drake flinched, a muscle ticking on his square jaw. He looked stricken for a second before he went blank again.

She saw that she'd managed to sneak into his armor.

Anya was glad. She was fiercely glad that she'd managed to hurt him. Make him feel a fraction of the devastation inside her. It soothed the damage done to her.

"Will you, Mr. Fallahil?" Her throat was scraped raw but she wouldn't allow him the satisfaction of breaking down.

Drake nodded, reluctantly. "If that's what you need."

"I don't…" She worked her throat till it would hold her tears. "I don't need anything from you. Except to leave me alone."

"As you wish." He inclined his golden head.

Anya backtracked from the room, keeping him in her sights, because she did not want him to think she was running from him.

No, she was choosing to leave on her own two feet. Her spine ramrod straight and her eyes utterly clear. And if her pride, self-worth and finer feelings lay in tatters at his feet, it was her secret to carry to the grave.

Anya left Drake the same way she'd entered his life. With her heart intact at the cost of her pride. Or so she told herself. Because the alternative was a truth too horrible to contemplate.

She called Swati in the bathroom with surprisingly calm hands.

"Hello, Anya," Swati began warmly. "How are you, beta?"

Anya's lips trembled before she firmed them up ruthlessly. "I'm fine, mama. I just wanted to call you and let you know…" She hesitated for a second. "I'm coming home. To take care of you."

She pressed end on the call before her mom could say another word and shatter Anya's fragile calm into a million pieces.

Drake and Anya's explosive, heartbreaking story continues in KEEP. Read on for an excerpt from KEEP.

KEEP

Ruthless Billionaires

"For a new bride, you look like shit, sis," Ishqi said bluntly as she wandered a shady pawn shop off Orchard Street, that weekend. She took a deep drag of the vape pen she carried. "God, I missed this. Are you done, Anya?"

Anya pocketed the hefty roll of dollars the pawn broker handed her. "Thank you, *ah-ma*." She told the kindly, white-haired matron minding the store. "I'm so glad you liked my pieces."

"This sapphire alone is worth ten times what I gave you, lah. Are you sure you don't mind waiting a few days?" Mama Jong asked Anya again, as she had thrice before. "My son says he'll contact the bank tomorrow and get you more funds."

Anya shook her head, so violently she almost gave herself whiplash. "No. I need the money now. Thank you so much for your kindness, Mama Jong. And you." She gave her sister a sharp look. "The sign clearly says No Smoking, Ishqi."

Ishqi waved her vape pen around, leaving a trailer of hot cinnamon vapor. "I'm not."

She looked like an angry fairy in her rainbow shorts and Doc Martens over fishnet stockings with a baby tee shirt and purple suspenders. The first thing she'd done once she'd been let out of jail yesterday was use Swati's emergency credit card and get herself spa'd up.

Her pixie-cut hair was now a curling purple mess, while an inch thick coal black mascara coated her fake lashes.

"Are you crying, Anya?" Ishqi asked curiously.

Anya shook her head, as the wet haze passed. As quickly as it had come. It came without warning over the last few days. Threatening to swallow her whole where she stood sometimes. And, each time, it was more difficult to wrest her control back so she wouldn't.

It came without warning ever since…

"No," Anya answered quietly. "I'm not a new anything, Ishqi, so stop saying that, will you?"

Ishqi shrugged. "Fine by me. I was just making polite conversation. I won't bring it up again."

They exited the dingy store full of collectibles and curios and emerged into a side street. It was almost afternoon, so the restaurants and pubs on the other side of the street were full of patrons.

Life was buzzing as it usually did on the weekends.

Ishqi bounced on the balls of her feet. "Can we grab something to eat, Anya? I don't want to make mom cook something specifically, since you're not coming back with me. I'm starving for some real *nasi goreng lemak*." She even added an urchin-like smile which melted Anya's heart.

Usually.

But now the idea of spooning in the spicy ramen noodle soup was enough to churn Anya's stomach. "Can we get it to go?" She smiled back. "I have some work to wrap up and I was hoping to get a jump start on next sem's course reading."

"I guess that's fine."

Ishqi dashed across the street, her ironic Hello Kitty backpack bouncing on her pert back.

Anya caught a sight of her own reflection in one of the restaurant glass walls. She looked like a ghost – in her all black tee and jeans outfit. Her hair severely pulled back in a braid, not a speck of makeup on her face. In fact, nothing on her face.

No animation. No color at all.

He'd actually drained her of color. That bastard.

Anya hurried and followed Ishqi into the restaurant. Because she had come very close to breaking her silent promise to herself.

She would not think of Drake Fallahil anymore. Not for a second.

He did not deserve it.

He deserved less than nothing from her, actually. Least of all the gift she'd given him without bothering to weigh the consequences.

It was the reason she'd pawned every single piece of jewelry he'd ever given her, the wedding ring, the sapphire necklace, and his expensive phone, just two weeks ago, with no compunction.

The money had been used to pay for the lawyer's retainer for Ishqi, resulting in her case being expedited and she'd actually been let out early for good behavior, pending further investigation.

She'd have given the clothes away too but she didn't want some other poor unfortunate woman to wear them and experience the same nightmare she was living. So she'd packed them into a trash bag and left it in the trash chute of the penthouse the second she'd cabbed back from the disastrous scene at his office.

She'd have moved out of his very orbit but she'd signed her name on the dotted line and pride demanded she stay put.

Besides, the fucking bastard hadn't bothered to as much as text her after she'd fled his office. He could be in Outer Mongolia for all she cared now.

Ishqi shook Anya's shoulders. So hard that her teeth rattled. She looked annoyed. "You want bubble tea to go with your *lemak*?"

Anya shook her head. "No, thanks, honey. I'm not hungry. You get whatever you want."

Ishqi held a palm out.

Anya stared at her. "What?"

"We have to pay for the food, don't we? I forgot to get mom's card and I'm not adding this to my payment app." She smiled sweetly. "This is your treat."

Anya handed over a few bills to Ishqi and exited the restaurant. It was beginning to make her feel like the walls were caving in. She leaned against one of the graffiti-ed walls and gulped in deep breaths.

~ ~ ~ ~ ~ ~ ~

The expression on Ishqi's face right now was the same as Drake's had been. As her mom always had.

This ridiculous hope that Anya would make everything better. She'd fix everything by breaking herself into two. Because they were *special* and she wasn't, so her only job was to accommodate them.

Her mom had depended so heavily on her till the operation and discarded her when she'd learned to stand on her own two feet. Ishqi was always self-centered, almost to the point of oblivion. Only, now Anya could see it so clearly. It was appalling.

Her sister only cared about herself. She'd not even bothered to thank Anya for the food or the fact that she'd paid for the lawyer's fees with jewelry she'd been given by her husband. She *expected* Anya to clean up her mess.

And *her fucking husband* was the worst of all. The worst offender.

He'd known the truth. He'd kept it from her. He'd not lied to her but what he'd done was worse.

Drake had used her.

Over and over.

And, the sorriest part was, for one second when he'd looked stricken… when he'd wanted to explain the truth to her, she wanted to listen to him. She'd *wanted* him to be different. Someone who cared about her, first.

But he wasn't.

Anya wasn't special. He'd wanted her to accommodate his special life at the cost of her own pride and self-worth.

And she was *damned* if she'd do it for him. No matter how he made her feel. No matter how she felt every time she *moved,* as if she could still feel him – thick and hard and perfect – inside her. Feeding her damned soul with his power. With him.

She hated herself most of all because she'd trusted this man to be safe. To be different. When he'd shown her, over and over again, that he was the literal devil incarnate.

Selfish. Depraved. Unconscionable.

~~~~~

Her phone, her old phone, buzzed. She answered without bothering to see the caller. "Yes, hello?"
~~~~~

"Anya?" Mili Iyer's sympathetic tones floated through the call. "Are you crying?"

"No. What?" She gritted out.

Anya touched a hand to her cheek. It came away sopping wet. She discovered she'd slouched almost to the ground with the force of her tears. Her epiphanies.

"Oh my god." She looked at her glistening hand. "I am crying."

Mili cursed stridently. "I am going to kill Drake when I see him. If ever."

Anya flinched. "I don't want to hear his name," she bit out. "Ever. Again."

"I know, love. I'm so sorry." Mili sounded so sympathetic, pitying even.

Anya wanted to scream at her to stop. But none of this was Mili's fault. She'd told Anya the truth about Drake the second they'd met.

He always got his way.

And look where not remembering it had gotten Anya.

"It's okay." She wiped her streaming face briskly. "What's up, Mili? Is there a problem with the projections I created for the new fund?"

"No," Mili answered slowly. "The Verdant Fund set up is done so perfectly, Anya. You have a real knack for cutting through the bullshit and explaining the logic behind the money. It's unlike anything I've ever seen. And I hate doing these decks so, thank you twice over."

The project was a hypothetical set up for structuring a Green Fund, where the investors and promoters were committed to using the money to mitigating climate change through alternative resources. Rerouting projects such as space exploration, tech innovation, mass production to something that would not kill the remaining forty percent of rainforests.

In fact, over the course of working on the project, Anya had become privy to the many ways, big and small, Fallahil Inc. supported and championed causes decidedly anti-capitalist in nature.

Drake had bought mammoth tracts of forest land in Asia, especially South East and South, and South America, and was reforesting it, acre by acre. His companies paid women equal wage, sexual harassment cells trickled down to the ground level, with legal action being levied immediately if ever someone was found abusing their power.

Not to mention what he'd done for the freaking Rhinoceres Project, single-handedly pouring millions into it to procure the necessary permits to mate the last remaining rhinoceros with a female.

She'd actually stumbled across a memo that Drake had written about the core seven hundred startups he'd invested in, where female hiring was at an all-time high and how the lack of a turnover had resulted in increased profits. It was a feminist manifesto couched in economic value.

She'd hardened her bruised heart each time she'd read about yet another silent contribution the man had made to further the cause of an ism, by remembering what he'd told her.

All of it was for profit, for business.

It had worked. Or, so she liked to think.

Anya smiled. "Working on this set up saved my sanity, so I have to thank you, Mili. But if that's not why you're calling, what's up?"

Mili was quiet for a long moment. "Drake called me from Australia where he's been in meetings for the last two weeks, you know."

"So?" Anya was cold, queenly. "What's it got to do with me?"

She didn't care about him anymore, not that she ever had. Beyond interning at his vastly interesting company.

She did not absolutely care that the fucking *cowardly* bastard had fled the country the same night she'd left the penthouse and stayed away in a poor imitation of a decent person. She wished he'd done that the first night they'd met.

"Well, he wants…Can I just read the message he sent me so you don't hate me for being in the middle of this?"

"Don't worry, Mili. I already know he's responsible for the mountains rising and the seas boiling," Anya reassured her. "I am not going to shoot the messenger. Although, I have to wonder. Why does someone who has a Harvard MBA and a Yale Law degree work for this despicable jerk?"

"Because," Mili sighed. "Very occasionally, almost without wanting to, he saves the damn world from burning down."

And other times he wrecks it.

Anya kept her harsh words to herself. "Read the message," she instructed. "Let's get this over with."

"Sending a charter jet for you for Saturday night. Have to attend AllMart CEO's wedding to the MD. Attendance is mandatory. – Drake."

Anya blinked. "What…what is happening?" She knew of AllMart. Any B-school student knew of the chain of departmental stores across Midwest US, headquartered in Chicago and helmed by Zara Subramanian, one of the youngest CEOs ever.

Mili sighed, loud and clear. "Drake's sister's sister-in-law is getting married. You both are invited to the wedding. It's in Chicago. And, attendance…"

"Is mandatory."

"Anya, I'm so *sorry*." Mili was distressed.

But Anya wasn't. She was filled with cold, righteous purpose. The melancholy and endless grief eating away at her was receding slowly under this new clarity. She didn't think about the instant of poisonous ache under her heart when she heard the word's *Drake's sister.*

The man had an actual family, instead of coming out as the devil spawn she knew him to be.

She focused instead on the fact pertaining to her.

Drake had done something she didn't expect him to do. Something she'd thought not possible.

Something that gave her freedom to do what she had to. Make him pay a thousand times over for the way he'd treated her.

Drake had broken his word and reneged on his deal. He'd not left her alone.

Now, she could do the same.

She was going to go be the world's worst bride at this wedding that was important to Drake and make him pay.

"Mili," Anya murmured. "Can you take the rest of the afternoon off? I need help with my bridal trousseau."

Mili whooped. "Fuck yeah, sister. I'll do you one better. I'll bring the Black Amex Drake keeps locked up in the safe for special emergencies. Orchard Street had better watch out."

"Yes," Anya vowed. "Everyone had better watch out. Here comes the bride…"

ACKNOWLEDGMENTS

I'd like to thank quite a few people who made the writing of this book possible --

Priyanka Menon, who screwed my head on straight with the vax scene. Thanks, love. I adore you so much.

Bri Blackwood and Ivy Mason, two fantastic billionaire dark romance authors who held my hand and helped instil a new level of confidence in me. Thank you, fabulous ladies.

My incredible team, my family and friends, without whom I'm simply lost sometimes.

And lastly, Aarti's Awesome ARCsters, bookstagrammers, and every single reader friend. Your love and support buoys me, keeps me going, and makes all the aches and pains worth it. I'm so lucky to have you so I can do this, all day every day.

The show Ishq Par Zor Nahin. My mom's obsessed with this series and so I wrote the heroine, Ishqi, of the show into Drake and Anya's story! Hope you like this birthday gift, mama.

ABOUT THE AUTHOR

Hi, there I'm Aarti V Raman. I write all shades and forms of romance or will in the future because I suffer from writing attention deficit disorder. I must tell all the stories! So, my romances range from romantic comedy, chick lit to romantic suspense and dark romance starring tortured billionaires and suffering military types!

Before I turned to writing and telling these stories full-time, I was a teacher, business journalist and editor for close to fifteen years. So my heroines are career-minded, city-living, strong-willed hot messes who still have their lives together. I believe in writing what I know and I know me best so most of these heroines are Indian (South Asian women of color).

I also believe in writing more of what I want so my heroes are indecently hot, filthy rich, fiendishly smart with secret hearts of gold. Thus, the angst and steam-meter are off the charts when stubborn force meets immovable object on the way to happy ever after. So does the banter and danger, because what's love without a little bit of jeopardy, am I right?

I'm a TEDx speaker and 22 of my romances have hit the Amazon Bestseller Charts so I can proudly call myself an Amazon 100 International Bestselling Author. My chick lit dramedy "The Worst Daughter Ever" has been optioned for screen. My bestselling Millionaire Foes series is part of the Writers on the Moon Project, on a time capsule to go to the actual moon.

I'm also known as Writer Gal. I live in Mumbai with my large and largely loveable extended family in a version of my three favorite words – Happy Ever After.

www.ingramcontent.com/pod-product-compliance
Lightning Source LLC
Chambersburg PA
CBHW050320160726
48002CB00001B/109